DI199896

Strong

Also from Kylie Scott

It Seemed Like a Good Idea at the Time

Trust

THE DIVE BAR SERIES
Dirty
Twist
Chaser

THE STAGE DIVE SERIES
Lick
Play
Lead
Deep

THE FLESH SERIES
Flesh
Skin
Flesh Series Novellas

Heart's a Mess

Colonist's Wife

Strong

A Stage Dive Novella
By Kylie Scott

1001 Dark Nights

EVIL EYE
CONCEPTS

Strong
A Stage Dive Novella
By Kylie Scott

Copyright 2018 Kylie Scott
ISBN: 978-1-948050-19-7

Published by Evil Eye Concepts, Incorporated

This is a work of fiction. Names, places, characters and incidents are the product of the author's imagination and are fictitious. Any resemblance to actual persons, living or dead, events or establishments is solely coincidental.

Sign up for the 1001 Dark Nights Newsletter
and be entered to win a Tiffany Key necklace.

There's a contest every month!

Go to www.1001DarkNights.com to subscribe.

As a bonus, all subscribers will receive a free copy of
Discovery Bundle Three
Featuring stories by
Sidney Bristol, Darcy Burke, T. Gephart
Stacey Kennedy, Adriana Locke
JB Salsbury, and Erika Wilde

One Thousand and One Dark Nights

Once upon a time, in the future...

*I was a student fascinated with stories and learning.
I studied philosophy, poetry, history, the occult, and
the art and science of love and magic. I had a vast
library at my father's home and collected thousands
of volumes of fantastic tales.*

*I learned all about ancient races and bygone
times. About myths and legends and dreams of all
people through the millennium. And the more I read
the stronger my imagination grew until I discovered
that I was able to travel into the stories... to actually
become part of them.*

*I wish I could say that I listened to my teacher
and respected my gift, as I ought to have. If I had, I
would not be telling you this tale now.
But I was foolhardy and confused, showing off
with bravery.*

*One afternoon, curious about the myth of the
Arabian Nights, I traveled back to ancient Persia to
see for myself if it was true that every day Shahryar
(Persian: شهريار, "king") married a new virgin, and then
sent yesterday's wife to be beheaded. It was written
and I had read, that by the time he met Scheherazade,
the vizier's daughter, he'd killed one thousand
women.*

Something went wrong with my efforts. I arrived in the midst of the story and somehow exchanged places with Scheherazade – a phenomena that had never occurred before and that still to this day, I cannot explain.

Now I am trapped in that ancient past. I have taken on Scheherazade's life and the only way I can protect myself and stay alive is to do what she did to protect herself and stay alive.

Every night the King calls for me and listens as I spin tales. And when the evening ends and dawn breaks, I stop at a point that leaves him breathless and yearning for more. And so the King spares my life for one more day, so that he might hear the rest of my dark tale.

As soon as I finish a story... I begin a new one... like the one that you, dear reader, have before you now.

CHAPTER ONE

"I don't believe this," I bitched. "My Valentino boots are actually sticking to the floor. That's how gross this place is."

Lizzy just smiled. "Told you to dress casual."

"I am."

The smile widened.

"Jeans and a tee is casual."

"A tee? It's velvet, Martha." She held a bottle of beer up to her lips, taking a sip. "I said we were going to a dive bar. You have only yourself to blame for the fashion faux pas."

"But velvet is in!"

"Would you two quit talking? I'm trying to listen," said my brother, Ben. The big hairy idiot was slouched back in his chair, bopping his head in time to the music.

Lizzy shuffled closer all conspiratorial-like. "I know why you're all dressed up."

I said nothing. There was nothing to be said.

Next her gaze went to the man standing at the end of the bar across from us. No, no, I would not turn my head. I would not fall prey to her bullshit. After all, I'd managed to successfully avoid him for the forty-eight or so hours since my not so triumphant surprise return to the West Coast. Even with us both being in the same house. A very big sprawling house, but still.

On the other hand, it should probably be mentioned that he looked awfully good tonight in jeans and a white T-shirt with a leather jacket. Samuel Rhodes, otherwise known as Sam. Not a pretty man with his harsh features and bull-like neck, but something about him appealed to me. As always, his head was shaved and his body was built and my idiot fingers itched to explore.

Okay. So I guess at some point I must have turned my head. And shit, he caught me looking.

The corner of his lips rose just a little, just enough to mess with me, before he returned to doing his job by casually surveying the packed room. My heart did not speed up due to anything done by him. Clearly, I hadn't totally caught my breath from when we'd walked in half an hour ago or something. That was all. Interesting to note, he did none of the checking me out typical of a heterosexual male who might have been into me. In fact, he didn't really give me any signals at all. Ever.

What did the odd almost smile mean? Not a hell of a lot. It wasn't like he ran around all of the time anyway. Sam tended to be kind of scary as per the job description. No, Lizzy had to be wrong, the man did not have a thing for me. A small amount of chemistry and weirdness didn't amount to a whole hell of a lot. Not if he wasn't willing to act on it. Because God knows I wasn't about to, not with my convoluted romantic history.

"Ooh, busted," said Lizzy. "The bodyguard caught you looking."

"Shut it." I inched my chin up a bit, trying not to frown because frowning gave you lines. "Sam and I have known each other for years and nothing has ever happened. You're completely wrong about this."

"Am I?"

"Yes, there's nothing between us."

"So that's why you were staring at him?"

I chose not to answer that. "And you know he prefers to be called executive protection officer instead of bodyguard."

At this, Lizzy burst out giggling, a malicious glee in her eyes. No wonder I liked my sister-in-law these days.

Ben shot us both an irritated glance. We both ignored it.

Of course, I'd known Sam would probably be here. Rock stars going out in public could be a delicate thing. People had a tendency to get overexcited. And while one person wanting an autograph wasn't a problem, twenty or thirty of them suddenly swarming definitely could be. Having once been part of the entourage, I'd seen it happen to Ben and his fellow Stage Dive band members enough times to be wary. And you couldn't get by with ordinary security. Rock stars needed protection from their over-zealous fans, but on the other hand they didn't want the fans roughed up or hurt in any way. It required a delicate balance: control, experience, and a whole gamut of scary physical skills. Hence Sam.

Still, Portland seemed generally less crazy than the good old days back in LA. All of the guys seemed calmer and more settled away from the constant craziness of the party scene. Not to mention the effect of all of the wives/partners and various offspring. The biggest rock band in the world had officially been domesticated.

It was kind of cute. Or sad. I don't know.

"Sorry, I didn't mean to stir you," she lied. "What do you think of your brother's new musical bromance?"

On the small stage set up in the corner of the room, a young man wailed his heart out while playing an acoustic guitar. Much angst about a girl who only called him after midnight. Trust a rockster to turn a simple booty call into a heartbreaking ballad. The song was damn good though. He had talent. If only I hadn't had my fill of the type when I was younger. The kid looked to be in his early to mid-twenties. Lanky with lots of tattoos. Your typical rock 'n roll Prince Charming. Gag. These days my type ran more toward…actually, what I needed or wanted in a male was a total mystery.

And my gaze did not stray back to Sam. That did not happen.

"He's not bad," I said, staying on topic. "And his stage presence is good, which is where the money is nowadays. So there's that, at least."

"Not bad?" Ben scoffed. "He's fucking brilliant."

With a smile, Lizzy held up her hands, making a heart shape out of her fingers.

"I saw that," grunted her husband.

"Adam is the new musical genius." She held her beer up to her lips again, downing a mouthful. "He's moving into our pool house because his cruel and vicious girlfriend kicked him out for being more into music than spending time with her. He's been sleeping on friends' couches ever since, poor boy."

I shook my head mockingly. "*Women.*"

"We ruin everything, right? What is even wrong with us?"

"Where to begin…we could be here for a while…"

Ben bit back a smile. "Go easy. He's young, be plenty of time for him to date and shit later."

"*And shit*," repeated Lizzy. "The pure romance of it hurts my soul."

"I'll give you romance."

On account of his size, my brother could just lift his wife out of her chair and deposit her on his lap. His hands went into her hair and their mouths met, the man kissing the life out of her. God, the amount of tongue going on and in public too. Married people. Couples in general. I could really do without having to see this sort of thing. Only when I turned away, Sam was watching me with what might almost be interest. What did the look in his eyes mean? I wish I knew. Something on the cell phone in his hand distracted him and our brief staring competition ended.

Up on stage, Adam the tortured musical genius finished his song and the room broke out into applause, whistling, hooting, and hollering. He certainly had the audience in the palm of his hand. With the right guidance, he'd go far.

Finally, much saliva later, my brother and sister-in-law came up for air. Nice to see their marriage was going strong. I'd been a disbeliever, but it was actually good to be proven wrong. They were both still stupidly romantic and happy. Must be nice for some.

"They love him," I said.

Ben nodded. "Adrian's interested in signing him."

"Shit human. Great manager."

"We don't use him for his winning personality."

"True enough." I nodded. "You're letting this guy move in with you? Isn't that a bit risky? What do you actually know about him?"

"Sam's checked him out. It's fine. And it's not like the place isn't big enough."

"True."

Music filled the room once more, the strumming of guitar strings and distant thump of the guy's foot hitting the floor. It was when Adam opened his mouth that the magic really happened, though. The boy could sing.

"Hey," said another voice...one I knew far too damn well. David Ferris, lead guitarist, head song-writer, and my ex, slipped into the seat Lizzy had so recently vacated beside me. Like the one on stage, he was long and lean. Beautiful in his own way. We kind of froze at the same time, exchanging pained looks. So much messy ugly history between us.

Young love gone wrong with cheating involved. My fault, not his. I liked to think that since then I'd lived, learned, and grown, etcetera, given it all happened a decade ago. But mostly, I'd just lived. In particular, I'd lived by never letting myself come even close to falling in love again. Love and I clearly didn't mix if it made me lose my mind and do dumb things. Maybe that counts as learning. Two out of three ain't bad.

"Martha," he said.

"Hi, David." My smile felt so brittle it almost hurt. "How are you?"

"Good. You?"

I just nodded.

Pleasantries exchanged, he shifted the chair back a bit from me and focused on my brother. "Benny, this the one you wanted me to hear? He's good."

"Yeah, was talking to him earlier. I'm going to produce his album, get him started."

"Cool."

"Got the equipment there, figure we might as well use it," said my brother. "Keep busy while you take some down time and work on the next album."

"I think it's a great idea."

Lizzy gave me something between a worried/sorry type look. God, I so didn't need that. David and I had been finished a long, long time ago. While my heart no longer broke at the thought of him, the sight of him wasn't exactly welcome. I mean, why would anyone want to revisit some of their worst moments? Sure there'd been some good ones in there too, but still. At least he hadn't brought his wife.

And what I needed right now was some space. "The ice has melted in my drink. I'm getting another."

"Do you want me to come too?" asked Lizzy.

"No, it's fine."

Movements stiff and awkward, I made my way through the crowd. Some interested gazes from strangers tracked over me, but I ignored them all. Flirting and what might follow wasn't high on my list of interests right now. Luckily, the bar wasn't far. The place might be packed, but the air-con was pumped up so my makeup hadn't melted off. Thank goodness. I'd been waiting at the bar for all of about point five of a second when Sam appeared alongside me. First hint he didn't need a drink, he was facing the wrong way, his gaze still on Ben, David, and the crowd. Second hint was when he opened his mouth and said, "Are you okay?"

"I'm fine."

He tipped his chin.

I scowled in return. "Do you need something?"

"Nope."

"Shouldn't you be working then?"

The sly sort of curve of his mouth happened again. "No need to switch on bitch mode just because someone expresses concern for you, Martha."

"Who said I ever turned it off?"

His smile broadened almost imperceptibly. I watched it happen out of the corner of my eye.

"Good to see the years spent in New York haven't changed you any," he said.

Not too sure about that.

"I was surprised to hear about your return."

"Spur of the moment type thing."

He just nodded, eyes now narrowed on me slightly. Like he could read my mind or something. Heaven help me if he could.

Valentino boot tapping against the hideous sticky beer-stained floor, I scowled some more. Something about the man just brought up my hackles. Like I couldn't afford to have a soft underbelly. Ever. He knew too much. "Sam, this place is gross."

"It's not so bad."

"Don't you hate having to wait around all the time?"

"I'm not waiting, I'm working," he said. "It's a plus he's good." He nodded toward the young man on stage.

"Developing an ear for talent, are we?"

"I'll leave that to Ben and Dave. And you." He leaned back against the bar. "Still remember that time you picked Jimmy Page playing on that Texas punk album. That blew everyone away. Davie didn't know whether to be proud of you, or jealous as hell that his girlfriend had picked it before he had."

I tried to keep my smile from showing. "It was nothing really."

"Nothing? For the next month Mal thought you had freaky musical powers and he'd shut up awestruck every time you opened your mouth. Anything that can silence that man is something to write home about."

It was nice of Sam to remember, even if it was just a little thing, long ago. Some time after Stage Dive's first album. Mal had been getting into Texas punk, of all things. With his usual irrepressible enthusiasm, he'd play air-drums to his mix-tape non-stop on the tour bus. Jimmy's always hated punk and wasn't shy about expressing his opinion, which of course just made Mal double down on it. Texas punk became all we ever heard.

Truth be told, the music was actually pretty good. But no way would I admit as much to Mal. Don't feed the animals. That's my motto when it comes to dealing with crazy drummers.

But this guitar track just came out of nowhere, somewhere in the middle of the mix tape. Hypnotic and melodic, but woven seamlessly into this frenzied, fast-paced cacophony. Breathtaking. Me being me, I'd said something totally inappropriate, like, "No way some garage band nobody plays guitar like that." Mal had fetched me the album cover, and sure enough it turned out the lead singer had sent the song to a friend in a band he'd once opened for, who had liked it enough to lay down a guitar track, and sent it back.

The friend was Jimmy Page. A year or two before he formed Led Zeppelin. Ain't rock 'n roll a crazy thing?

Sam lingered, still smiling at the memory, and shaking his head. I blushed a little, wishing that his esteem for me didn't matter quite as much. Time to steer the conversation back to safer terrain. "So why do you say he's good then?"

He shrugged modestly. "You can hear talent. I can read a room. Ninety percent of this job is situational awareness and threat assessment. He's got them eating out of the palm of his hand. Makes life easy for me."

That made sense. "But what if Ben and Dave get recognized?"

"A couple of people have spotted them already, but they've been content to leave them be. It helps that the kid on stage is keeping the crowd occupied. But if the atmosphere changes, I'll get them out the back and Ziggy will have the car waiting."

"Is that what the phone is for?" I asked, nodding at the cell in his hand.

"We're keeping in contact."

"You're all prepared."

"That's what I'm paid for."

"And here I was thinking you were just hired muscle to make them look important."

"You think Dave needs me to look important?" Ouch. I take a shot at Sam's work, he twists my words around to target my old injury. Sometimes I wonder how much he sees the world as a perpetual sparring session. Always reading the situation, finding vulnerabilities, turning defense into attack. And always in control.

His gaze slipped to the side. "Bartender's waiting to take your order."

"Hmm? Oh." I turned, getting my thoughts in order. "Vodka and soda."

Sam clicked his tongue. "Manners."

"Please," I simpered. The woman behind the bar just raised a brow, hands already busy making up my order.

"It wouldn't kill you to be nice to people, Martha."

"Why risk it?" I handed the woman a ten-dollar bill, the cost of the drink and a healthy tip, thank you very much. Proof I could be nice in the ways that mattered. But Sam had already wandered back to his post by the end of the bar, within closer range of the guys.

Time to go back to the table. Kill me now.

I pasted a smile on my face and pushed my way back through the crowd. If any bastard spilled booze on my boots I'd maim them. It wasn't like I had the money to replace them these days.

Lizzy still sat in Ben's lap, leaving my chair next to David free. Yippee. As soon as I sat down, his jaw firmed in a certain way. Fuck. He was going to try to make conversation. I really wished he wouldn't. "So, Martha, how long are you in town for?"

"Haven't decided yet." I took a healthy gulp of vodka. Magical potato juice was definitely required.

"She's going to help look after Gib while Lizzy starts back at school," provided Ben. "We hadn't found a nanny we were happy with yet, so…"

"I'm delighted to be filling in."

David's forehead filled with worry lines. "You're going to look after a two-year-old? You?"

"She's going to be great!" Lizzy couldn't have smiled any brighter or less convincingly if she tried. "Excellent bonding time between aunty and nephew."

"Exactly," I agreed. "Anyway, how hard can it be?"

"What do you know about children?" asked David. "I mean, you couldn't even keep a mouse alive."

"That wasn't my fault." This was the problem with associating with people who'd known you during your childhood. "It got sick."

"You killed a mouse?" Lizzy's expression morphed to something much less confident.

Ben scratched at his beard. "I'd forgotten about that."

"Only reason you remembered to feed it and give it water was because I reminded you every day," said David, who really needed to fuck off right about now. Not helpful at all. Not that I expected him to be.

"I would have remembered eventually." A headache was coming on, I could feel it. "I was sixteen. Everyone's useless when they're sixteen."

"So what was your excuse for the following decade then?" Ben snickered at his own genius.

In true sisterly fashion, I thumped him in the arm. Mostly it just hurt my hand, the muscly bastard. Family and exes sucked. Maybe I should just go back to New York. Out of nowhere, a shiver worked its way down my spine. Nope. New York wasn't an option.

"I'm sure you'll be fine," said my brother, patting me on the head. Like it hadn't taken me quality time to get the slicked-back ponytail just right. The idiot. "Sorry, Martha. I have confidence you won't let my child die like you did the poor innocent mouse. May it rest in peace."

Meanwhile, open alarm filled the child's mother's eyes at the jokes.

"Nothing will happen to Gibby, I promise," I said, grabbing her hand. "You trust me, don't you?"

"Sure. Of course." And that did not sound convincing. Her giving my brother a worried glance didn't boost my confidence either. Perhaps this was a bad idea. I was a hell of a long way from Mary Poppins. Even if I did happen to love the kid in question.

"Sweetheart, it'll be fine." Ben kissed her on the cheek, tightening his hold. "Seriously, relax. We're just giving Martha shit. But she's a mature responsible adult and I'll be right there in the house if there's a problem. Sam will be there too. There'll be plenty of people around to help out if need be."

"Okay." This time her smile didn't seem quite so panicked at least. I wished it hadn't taken the mention of Sam to ease her mind about my inability to look after her child. But such was life.

Shoulders squared and tits out, I presented my most confident face. "I can do this."

CHAPTER TWO

"You've got yogurt in your hair."

"He threw it at me." Shoulders slumped, I sat on the carpet, some godawful children's show blaring from the TV. "I can't do this. The kid hates me."

"Martha." Sam sighed. "He's two and a half and doesn't even know you. Give it a chance."

The he in question, Gibson Thunderbird Rollins-Nicholson, stared rapt at the screen as animated dogs pulled off a daring rescue. Crazy name for a little kid. Being born a musician's progeny clearly came with the risk of being named after their favourite instrument. Meanwhile, the executive protection officer leaned against a nearby wall with his arms crossed over his broad chest. A small towel was slung over one buff shoulder and he wore workout gear. Guess he'd been making use of the private gym.

Ben and Lizzy hadn't stinted on the place. A sprawling Georgian Colonial in one of the fancier areas of Portland. Of course, the former ballroom/indoor basketball court had been converted into a recording studio and band practice area. My brother only really cared about two things, music and family, so no big surprise about the remodelling. Not that I'd been counting on them throwing any large parties to keep me entertained. Those wild days of groupies, models, and film stars hanging around and swinging off the chandeliers were long gone. Probably for the best.

"David was right, I don't know a thing about children," I said, feeling deeply sorry for myself. "I figured I spent years running around after rock stars, catering to their every whim. How different could it be?

So he's shorter and doesn't know how to express himself particularly well. All Mal ever did was babble incoherently at me. Some days I basically had to wipe the drool off that maniac's chin. After him, Gibson should be a dream, right?"

"Not so much, huh?"

"Not so much."

"What's wrong with your eye? It's a bit red," he asked, leaning closer.

"Huh? Oh, it got yogurt in it too," I lied, turning away. "I've been rubbing it."

"Ah."

Thank goodness my thick makeup covered the rest of the mess. Sam plucked a Kleenex from a box nearby and wandered closer, inspecting my dairy product-splattered hair. The intoxicating scent of clean male sweat filled the air as he leaned in. His gray tank was faded and old. But good Lord, did it do amazing things regarding leaving the bulk of his arms on display. All of his skin glistened and my stomach tumbled and tightened. It felt almost like nerves. Though I did not have a crush on the man. Because how ridiculous would that be?

His hand came toward me and I flinched. Dammit.

The hand paused ever-so-briefly and even with my eyes askance, I could feel his gaze drilling into me, searching my face. *He can see it.* Of course he could see it. No amount of makeup was going to hide that sort of thing from Sam. Whatever else his virtues and vices, the man was good at his job. And his job was violence. Recognizing it, and knowing how to prevent it. Still, it grated on me to show any sign of weakness. I'd rather be an overly proud bitch than a weak and wounded little thing any day of the week.

Then the pause was over and the hand continued forward. "Just cleaning you up," he said, his voice deeper than the ocean.

"Yeah, I…" *Shit.* "Thanks."

Ever so carefully, he lifted a thick strand of my dark hair and wiped it clean. His movements were cautious and slower than usual. I ignored the way his brows had drawn in ever so slightly.

"Maybe I should start shaving my head like you do," I joked, disliking the way-too-loaded silence between us. "If he's going to make a habit of throwing food at me."

A manly grunt.

"Bet it cuts right down on the styling time and I'd save a bundle on shampoo."

"Sam-Sam-Sam-Sam-Sam." Gib threw himself at the big man's back, little arms latching around his thick neck. Of course the kid loved him. It was just me he hated, his own flesh and blood. Lovely.

"Hey, buddy. You behaving yourself?"

Gib nodded his head up and down with much enthusiasm, the little fibber.

"Then why did poor Martha have yogurt in her hair?"

The kid just shrugged. "Want Mom."

"Your mom's at college. She'll be back later."

"Daddy?"

"He's busy working right now," said Sam in soothing tones. "You need to hang out with your Aunty Martha for a while. Your folks will be back soon, okay?"

"No!"

"Gibby—"

"No-no-no."

"He's big on repetition," I said, wincing at all of the noise. For little lungs, the boy sure was loud.

"You can have fun with Aunty Martha." Sam's smile was so hopeful. "Hanging out with Aunty Martha's great, isn't it, buddy?"

"No-no-no."

"Who could have guessed he'd say that?" I whispered. "Though to be fair, I'm kind of with him on that one."

One of Sam's brows arched, his gaze turning speculative. "You could be fun...in certain situations."

I shut my mouth tight before it even had a chance to hang open.

"If you wanted to be."

"Oh, really?" I cocked my head. "If I wanted to be in the situation or if I wanted to be fun?"

"Either. Both."

"Huh."

Gib patted Sam's thick shoulders all affectionate like. Damn. The man's muscles had muscles. How much time did he even spend in the gym? Not that he was preening or arrogant. I'd never met anyone less into worrying about what he looked like. It was all work-work-work for the man.

"What are the dogs up to today?" he asked Gib.

Immediately, the child raised his chin and "aroo-ed" at the top of his voice. As howls went, it was pretty spectacular. This task completed, he climbed off the big man and ran back to his former position standing in front of the TV.

Sam smiled. "Kids get pretty obsessed with shows. This one's been his favorite for a while."

"Talking dogs are pretty cool, I guess."

For a moment, he just stared at me.

"Have I still got yogurt in my hair?"

"No, I got it all out."

I nodded, turning my attention to my hands. It was easier than looking at him or dealing with all of the confusion his presence inspired. Time for a new manicure. One of my thumbnails was even chipped. To be fair, it kind of matched the whole food-fights-with-an-infant theme I had going on. Stylists and influencers would be so jealous.

"You never used to be nervous around me," he said quietly.

"Nervous around you? Seriously?" I scoffed. "Maybe if you weren't crowding me..."

The man didn't move an inch. Jerk. "We didn't get much of a chance to talk last night. What bought you back to the West Coast?"

"I wanted to see my family."

"That all?"

"Is that honestly so bizarre?"

"Combined with volunteering to look after Gib, it is a bit, yes."

I bit back the word *asshole*. Just. "What is this, an interrogation? Are you worried that I'm a security threat or something?"

"Of course not. My job is to make sure that everyone's safe," he said. "That they're okay. And that includes you. You're part of the family too."

"Well, thanks but no thanks for your professional concern. I'm fine."

He just looked at me.

"Don't you ever switch off from your job?" I asked.

"I'll switch off when the world's a safe place and nobody needs me around anymore. But we both know the world's not a safe place."

"That's very Superman of you, Sam. Anyway, I'm not sure I'll be around that long."

"Guess we'll see." He rose to his feet and without another word wandered off toward the hallway. Thankfully, Gib was too engrossed in his show to be paying attention to the somewhat awkward conversation. Not that I was intimidated by a small child or what he thought of me. Or of an executive protection officer's opinion, for that matter.

I was fine. Everything was fine. With a deep calming breath, I turned my hand, hiding the chip in my polish. I'd fix it later.

I stared mindlessly at the contents of my closet. The next job on my list of not particularly necessary things to do alone in my room. First had come the pedicure, facial, long soak in the tub while catching up on the entertainment industry news on my smart phone. Followed by eyebrow maintenance, some replying to emails, and my moisturizing routine. Now for this…how much exactly to unpack was the question. Outfits suitable for the New York party scene were less appropriate for wrangling small children and my previous work gear pretty much fell under the same category. None of it would stand up to the kind of rough usage a toddler could provide. Food fights. Shuffling around my knees picking up toys and such. Chasing after short, evil children on the run from their vegetables and bath time.

Fair to say I no longer quite recognized myself or my life. But I'd needed a job. More importantly, I'd needed to come home.

"Hey," said Lizzy, wandering in without knocking. Guess it sort of was her house. "What are you doing?"

"Just organizing myself." Caught out minus the heavy makeup, I kept my face angled down. Hopefully, with the low lighting, Lizzy wouldn't see anything.

"You didn't come down for dinner."

"Not hungry."

"You know where the kitchen is if you change your mind," she said. "We were going to watch some TV. Did you want to come join us?"

"Sort of busy right now," I hedged. Because while I might have reluctantly realized I needed to be around my family, actually giving in to the need was another thing entirely. "But thanks for asking."

"Okay. So long as you know you don't have to hide out in your room."

"I'm not *hiding*." I took in the baby monitor attached to my sister-in-law's waist and sighed. "Should I be wearing that?"

She snorted. "We don't expect you to be on duty twenty-four-seven, Martha. Sheesh."

I just shrugged.

"Is that how things normally go in your line of work?" Lizzy sat on the end of the bed, making herself comfortable.

"Mostly I do a mix of PR and executive assistant type functions. Usually for people with delicate egos, lots of money, and busy planners. Entertainment industry, mostly," I said. "Being summoned at four in the morning isn't unheard of."

"My baby boy can be high-maintenance all right. But any four in the morning nonsense can be handled by me or his father." She grinned. "Is the room okay?"

"Yes, it's lovely. Bigger than my whole apartment back in New York."

"Good. Glad you like it. We want you to be comfortable here."

I leaned back against the antique closet, arms crossed over my chest.

"Maybe you could even be comfortable enough to tell me about that bruise on your face sometime."

"Lizzy…"

"Don't worry," she said. "While I might be freaking out internally, I'm not going to push you for answers you're not ready to give. And I really am freaking the fuck out internally, FYI."

"Thank you for not pushing."

"Yet." Her shoulders rose on a deep breath as she took her time, obviously thinking over what to say next. How damn awkward. "Martha, your brother's missed you, you know? You're pretty much the only family he has."

"He's got the guys."

Lizzy shook her head. "It's not the same. You're his sister, he loves you, and we've barely even seen you since Gibby was born. Plus my child should have an aunt he can actually recognize on sight. That would be nice."

"Well, I'm here now."

"Yes, but for how long?" She eyed the still mostly packed suitcase sitting open on the floor. It was a mess. A fitting description for my life right now. "Come on, hang up your clothes, Martha. Settle in and give us a chance."

My laughter sounded brittle and false to my own ears. I doubted Lizzy would be swallowing it. The whole psychology degree thing had to get in the way. While she might not be grilling me about the black eye, her gaze kept returning to the ugly mark just the same. At least she wasn't showing me any pity or other such unwanted weirdness.

"I'm serious."

"Regardless of what it looks like, I don't need protecting. You can't really want me living here constantly in your face all the time," I said. "The house is big, but it's not that big. Trust me, it'll get old."

"Are you kidding? Since Jimmy and Lena moved and the studio got relocated to our place, it's been designated band headquarters. People are over all the time. It's a big part of why we got this place." She crossed her legs, kicking one foot idly. "Unless it's running into the guys all the time that has you worried."

I said nothing.

"And then there's Sam, of course."

Still nothing. My trap could have been wired shut.

"And all of the assorted wives."

"Are you seriously trying to head doctor me right now?" I asked. Her sudden smile was beatific, making it hard for me to hold on to the grumpy. Luckily, I had a lot of experience with being in a bad mood. "Please don't."

"Just because you have a complicated history with people doesn't mean you can't have positive future interactions with them." After my comment, she'd clearly decided to move into full-throttle psychologist mode. "Apologies and a little attitude adjustment can go a long way."

"Sweet baby Jesus, just strike me down," I said to the plain white ceiling. "Take me now."

"That's a lot to put on a baby, don't you think?"

"After chasing around your child all day, I believe he'd be up to the mission."

She smirked. "You see, Martha, I feel like we're not only sisters-in-law. But we have the potential for besties here and it would be a shame to see that potential wasted."

"Oh, do you now?"

"I do. And if nothing else, imagine how much it will irritate your brother to have us ganging up on him." At this thought, she outright evil-giggled. The woman's ability to tolerate no bullshit and yet still have fun was impressive.

"Valid point."

With all due grace, Lizzy rose to her feet and meandered over to the door. "Tell me you'll think about it."

I didn't say a word.

"Damn, you're stubborn. Just like your brother." She pushed my bedroom door wide open as if she was inviting the whole damn world in. "You're going to think about it and then you'll decide to stay. Imagine it, Martha, you won't have to be alone anymore."

I frowned, unhappy at the choice of words. "I'm not *alone* exactly. There were people I spent time with. Acquaintances I guess you could call them…and I was casually seeing someone for a little while."

Mouth shut, the woman just watched me. So much judgment in her eyes. How ridiculous. She couldn't possibly know no one had even bothered trying to call me since leaving the East Coast.

"I'll have you know I appeared on numerous society pages and influencers style blogs almost every other week. My life was very full until this little upset."

"Wow," she said flatly, obviously unimpressed. "So you basically had some fake friends, a dude you did it with once or twice, and a job that made insane demands on you and did your head in. What a full, rich, and complex life indeed."

"You didn't used to be this sarcastic."

"You didn't used to be this bruised."

I swore extra quietly beneath my breath. Guess spending time with a kid had already started to rub off on me. "Take your shrinking skills elsewhere. I do not need a therapist, Lizzy."

"No? What about a friend?" And with that parting shot, she was gone.

CHAPTER THREE

A moment, that's all it had taken. One short moment when I was deleting the bulk of my New York contacts off my phone and the child had disappeared. Of course the problem was, the great room where we generally hung out to watch dog cartoons on repeat and spread his huge collection of toys far and wide didn't have a door. Instead, it joined a hallway running the length of the house. The same hallway I now ran along looking for the short evil one. And we all know where he got the evil from. That's right, his mother. Not my side of the family. No way.

"Gib?" I called, looking into rooms as I passed. "Gibby, where are you?"

For two and a half days we'd gotten along okay, my nephew and I. Mostly due to my bribing him with his favorite foods. Chocolate chip cookies (made by the housekeeper who came in during the day, Greta), chicken nuggets, and grapes. A not completely unhealthy diet. After all, the five food groups were all roughly represented. Today, however, no amount of bribery worked. Gib was in a foul mood for some reason and hell bent on taking it out on me. Reminded me of a few years back when I'd been working for a big time fashion model and she'd thrown a next-season Louboutin at my head. Lucky me, we'd been the same shoe size. So it served her right that I caught the shoe and took its mate as an unspoken apology for the incident.

But back to child wrangling.

From the not-so-far distance, the sound of voices, the strumming of a guitar, and the tapping of a drumbeat drifted this way. It was like a rock 'n roll siren call. Especially to a two-and-a-half-year-old who pretty much wanted to hang out with anyone but me. "Oh no."

On account of the left hand side of the house where the studio and band practice area, games room, home theater, wine room, gym, sauna, and second kitchen (because didn't everyone need a second kitchen?) were located having its own entrance, I'd happily missed out on the bulk of all of the Stage Dive comings and goings. Even Sam lived in the two-bedroom pool house out back with Adam the musical genius. Apart from my needling head doctor of a sister-in-law and idiot brother, I'd pretty much kept to myself. Because there was nothing wrong with alone, no matter what Lizzy said. Alone was perfectly fine and actually quite safe. Especially given the bulk of the people who tended to visit the house.

And there they all were.

Jimmy sat sprawled on one of the leather sofas, watching his brother David, sitting on a large amp opposite him, tune a guitar. Mal, the blond-haired maniac, sat behind a drum kit, keeping up a relatively quiet though steady beat. And Gib was in his father's arms, safe and sound. Thank God.

I tightened my slightly sloppy ponytail and stood taller. Jeans and a tee wasn't my usual slick day wear. But at least there were currently no food groups represented in my hair.

"But you're supposed to hang out with Aunty Martha. We talked about this," said Ben with a frown. "What if she gets lost? She hasn't been here that long. She doesn't know the house like you do."

"Aunty Martha there." Expression decidedly unconvinced by the argument, Gib pointed at me, standing in the doorway.

I lifted a hand in greeting. "He got away from me."

Mal snorted, the jerk.

Ben just nodded. "Yeah, I noticed. He's like Houdini when he gets an idea into his head that he wants to be somewhere else. Kind of impressed you kept him occupied for as long as you did, actually."

Phew.

"Keeping track of children isn't as easy as it looks," said Jimmy with a small smile. Not a smirk, however, which was interesting. It might have almost been kind. Marriage and fatherhood must have mellowed him plenty.

"I'm finding that out," I said.

David just jerked his chin at me. Not awkward at all.

With an electric guitar in his hands, the new kid, Adam, stood waiting nearby. He looked a little wide eyed at the company he was keeping. Fair enough. Any no-name baby rocker like him would give up valuable parts of their anatomy to be hanging out with Stage Dive.

"What did you think?" he asked Ben, gaze hopeful yet braced for the worst.

Mal cleared his throat. "So you'd label that maybe a standard sort of rock, pop, soul, with a dash of Americana-type sound, yeah?"

Adam just blinked. "Ah, well—"

"Don't get me wrong. While there's nothing particularly fresh or interesting about what you're doing, you don't completely suck. Not completely," said Mal, all seriousness. "I hope you can find something to cling to in that, son."

"Ignore him," groaned David. "Unless you want to hit him with something. That's fine too."

"Hey!" Mal held up his drum sticks, making the symbol of the cross. "Stay back, fiends. I'm a ninja master with a set of sticks in my hands. I could take you all down without even raising a sweat."

A hand rubbing tiredly over his face, Ben nodded in agreement. "Definitely ignore him. God knows we do. Your sound is fine, Adam. In fact, it's damn good. That's why you're here."

Brows drawn tight, Adam looked around the room. "Okay."

Mal grinned. The man truly was the Puck or Loki of rock 'n roll. Pure mischief with a side order of annoying as all hell. "Actually, the truth is that you're killing it. But we hate any sort of genuine competition and the only way we could think of crushing your talent was to have Ben produce your next album."

Ben quietly grumbled something rude, given the small ears no doubt listening.

"So I've decided I'll play on your album, Adam. But like under a pseudonym," said Mal. "This is going to be great. I'll use a cool fake name like Captain P. Niss. Get it?"

"You're an idiot," said Jimmy flatly.

Surprisingly enough, the drummer actually looked vaguely wounded. "Anne thought it was hilarious."

"Your wife is an incredibly kind and gracious person."

"Enough. You can play uncredited," said Ben, ending the discussion.

"You can't hide talent that easily. The true musos will still recognize my style. They'll be like, 'no way that's anyone but Malcolm Ericson on the drums'. Tell them, Marty."

"Ben, you guys are working. Let me take him." Ignoring Mal, I wandered over to my brother, arms extended for the two-year-old terror. Gib of course scowled and turned away, hiding his face in his father's thick shoulder. Like I was the worst. Sigh. To think, I'd actually imagined he and I were bonding sort of over the last few days. Sure, it was based on an illicit chocolate chip cookie enticement system, but you had to start somewhere.

The doors to the outside pool and garden area opened, Sam slipping inside. Immediately, I tensed up further. This was just not my day.

"Done a full sweep of the surrounding area, Sam the Man?" asked Mal. "We under attack from rabid teenage girls again or what?"

The red had faded from my right eye, but I kept my face angled downward just the same. What with the amount of concealer I'd been using, no one could possibly see the bruising. Still, the bodyguard tended to notice things others didn't.

Sam's expression never slipped from his business-as-usual demeanour, regardless of the drummer's ribbing. God knows where he found the patience. Though he had been working with the band for years. Guess he was used to it by now. "A few fans and some paparazzi are hanging around the front gate. Ziggy's keeping an eye on them. Otherwise, you're as safe and sound as I can make you, Malcolm."

"Does that happen often?" asked Adam. "The rabid teenage girls thing?"

Sam shook his head. "Nah. Their fan base has grown up with them. These days, they're more likely to just want to have a chat and take a picture. It's the odd one who's unbalanced that we have to watch out for."

"Like the chick that broke into Jimmy and Lena's place last year. The woman used their shower then took a little nap in their bed," said Mal. "Crazy town."

Adam's eyes opened even wider.

"My bed I could have understood, but Jimmy's? That woman needs help." Mal paused, remembering. "Then there was the dude following me around last year and sending me poetry. He actually wasn't bad."

"How'd the one about your eyes go again?" Jimmy smirked.

"Don't get him started," groaned David.

With a heavy sigh, Mal smiled. "Yeah, it was all fun and games 'til he tried to rip some hair out of my head. I mean, I can understand where he's coming from, me being a sex god and all. But he scared the crap out of Anne. Pushed her out of the way to get to me. She could have been badly hurt."

Jimmy took in Adam's seriously alarmed expression. "That's about when we brought Ziggy and Luke on board to help Sam out," he said, in a soothing, nonchalant tone. "We always had a team on tour, but with wives and kids involved...better to be safe than sorry. They rotate between us, keeping an eye on things." Jimmy scratched at the stubble lining his jaw. "Plus Lena and I got a place with better security. Our daughters needed more space anyway, a bigger yard to play in and stuff like that."

"Oh, please, your old place was like a freaking mausoleum."

"It was not. That house won an architectural award."

"It was cold and ugly," said Mal. "Lena made you move, admit it. Your wife runs the show and she'd had enough of all the butt ugly monochrome and marble. That's the truth."

After first checking Gib wasn't watching, Jimmy flipped the idiot drummer the bird.

The small child, however, had already found something inappropriate to latch onto. "Butt! Butt-butt-butt!"

"Good work," grumbled Ben.

Mal laughed, spurring the kid on. Figures. They were both about the same maturity level.

"Are you sure you don't want me to take him?" I asked, one brow arched high.

Ben shook his head, setting Gibby down once he started wriggling, wanting to explore. With more shouts of "butt," he ran over to his Uncle Mal, who immediately set him up on his lap. A pair of kid-size earmuffs, no doubt hanging on the kit for this very reason, went on Gibby's head, and soon Mal was helping him wield the drum sticks. The resulting noise was without rhyme or rhythm and astonishingly loud. Made me wish Mal had earmuffs for the rest of us too. But at least Gibby had been distracted from yelling out any colorful language.

"Having second thoughts about the fame thing?" I asked Adam, wandering closer.

The young man shrugged. "I just want to play my music. What happens happens, you know?"

Sam stood in the corner, doing his silent sentry thing. Every now and then his gaze would take in the view of the pool outside, checking for anyone who didn't belong. With all of the guys gathered in the one place, security would be more intense than usual. Today he was wearing thick black boots, jeans, and a matching T-shirt. It suited him, the whole dark and dangerous thing he had going on.

I might have been somewhat distracted and lost track of the conversation when something caught my attention. "What did you say?"

Ben looked up. "I said Adrian's talking about getting Adam a place in the Mackee Festival line-up."

"That's a terrible idea."

"Why?"

"The festival's under new management and apparently they're clueless as all fu…fudge. Odds are it's going to be a disaster. What the hell is Adrian thinking?"

Jimmy cocked his head, watching me with interest for some reason.

"Just because I've been on the other side of the country doesn't mean I haven't kept up with industry news."

"So what would you recommend?" asked Ben.

It seemed like every set of eyes in the room was turned my way. I crossed my arms, feeling just a tiny bit defensive perhaps. "Festivals are a good idea, I'll give Adrian that. Help to establish Adam more widely and build on his audience. I'd definitely talk to Tyra about a place in the Newport and maybe the End of Summer and Rock 'n Waves. You're only interested in stateside at the moment, right?"

Adam gulped. "Ah, I guess?"

"He's so clueless, it's cute," laughed Mal. Amazing he could keep track of the conversation while helping Gib create chaos on the high hats.

And Jimmy was still watching me, which I so could have done without.

"What?" I scowled.

"Just a thought is all…" said Jimmy.

"What thought?"

From over by the windows, Sam watched me too, his bland business face morphing into something questioning for a moment. The weirdness in the room was seriously starting to get to me.

"Bet you've kept up with your contacts too, haven't you?" asked Jimmy. "Or it wouldn't take much to get up to date. You always were good at the schmoozing and getting people to do what you wanted. Had a hell of a talent for it, if I remember correctly."

Now even my brother joined in, his brows lifting in surprise. "Huh. Probably would never have occurred to me, but you're right, Jim. It's not a bad idea at all. Smart, organized, has experience or at least a working knowledge of pretty much every part of the industry."

"What the hell are you all talking about?" I barked.

"Hell!" yelled Gib, making me wince. Evidently I'd raised my voice enough to penetrate through the earmuffs. Though really on a scale of inappropriate words, it couldn't be worse than butt.

"She always did keep a close eye on everything. I mean, she was good at her job," said David, carrying on the discussion. Though his tone seemed distinctly reluctant when it came to doling out praise. "Sure this babysitting thing is really for you, Martha?"

"It's not a long-term solution, but it's all right for now. Why?"

Sam cleared his throat. "They're thinking you'd make a great manager for Adam. I happen to agree."

"A manager? Me?"

"Sure, why not?" Ben walked over to stand in front of me, his mouth a very straight and serious line. "You're your own kind of scary, just like Adrian is. But you're way better at smooth-talking people than he'll ever be. Adam could do a hell of a lot worse."

"I'm my own kind of scary?" I asked, one brow raised.

"You know you are," said Jimmy from over on the couch. "You're a hard ass from way back."

"All of this flattery is going to go to my head," I joked.

"Ass!" shouted Gib.

This time it was Ben who winced. "Liz's going to kill me. Look, Martha, just think about it, okay?"

"Shouldn't Adam get a say in this?"

The baby rocker looked around the room some more with his big innocent bewildered eyes. If nothing else, the boy would look great on the covers of magazines. Though his clothes and hair needed a bit of work. "I guess she seems nicer than Adrian?"

"Martha nice? You're hilarious," said Mal, setting Gibby down on the ground.

The child immediately ran over to the couch to climb up between David and Jimmy. Both held up their hands and some complicated game involving Gibby taking turns high fiving the two men began. It was kind of cute seeing them interact with him. How natural and relaxed they were these days with a small child in their midst.

"Anyway," continued Mal. "You don't want anyone too nice. It's an industry that'll chew you up and spit you out if you're not careful. You want someone like Martha who'll watch your back and cover your interests."

"Were you actually just praising me?" I asked, shocked.

One side of the maniac's mouth pulled upward. "Marty, darling…a move into management makes total sense. You might look pretty as a picture, but you're a natural bully and a thug. Always have been, always will be."

So many smirks and smiles filled the room. Even Sam covered a bark of laughter with the worst fake cough ever. Bastards. But I didn't flip out or fly into a rage. Instead, I took a moment to think the imbecile drummer's words over. "Actually, Malcolm, I'm going to take that as a compliment."

"I think you should." Ben slipped an arm around my shoulders, even going so far with the sibling affection as to kiss me on the cheek. "Martha?"

"Hmm?"

"You have a black eye," he said, the words strained.

Dammit. I'd been distracted, and let him get too close. A strange sort of silence filled the room and I immediately took a step away from him, covering the right side of my face with my hand. "It's fine. God, Ben, way to make a big deal out of it and embarrass me. I just bumped my…"

"No. Do not lie." He loomed over me, radiating anger. "How did that happen?"

My mouth shut tight, a stupid unnecessary panic filling my veins. For fuck's sake, this was my brother. No matter how upset he got, he wouldn't hurt me. But the need for fight or flight pressed at me.

"Ben, mate, take a step back. Give her some space." Sam's calm and steady voice came from my side. When he'd moved, I had no idea. But he'd obviously been fast. "You're scaring her. Look at her face."

"I am not afraid." My voice sounded about an octave higher than normal. "I'm not afraid of anything."

"Of course you're not," soothed Sam, his rough, familiar features oh so welcome. I don't know why his smile chilled me out, but it did. My shoulders inched back down and breathing came easier. "You're a fighter, aren't you, Martha? Now, why don't you tell us what happened to your face? And like your brother said, the truth please."

I sighed, turning my face away. "I got mugged."

Beside me, my brother seemed to swell with fury. "And you didn't think you should tell—"

"Ben," said Sam with unerring patience.

"Inside voices," shouted Gib, not the least bit ironically, before sticking his thumb in his mouth.

"That's right, Gibby." Sam nodded and smiled. "We're staying nice and calm and using our quiet inside voices while Aunty Martha tells her story, aren't we?"

The child nodded emphatically then crawled onto Jimmy's lap, obviously in search of comfort. All of the tension in the room must have had him worried. Without a word, the singer gathered him close, cuddling the small child and rubbing his back.

"Sorry." Ben slumped back against the wall, his face lined with concern. "I'll try and relax."

Sam turned back to me, waiting.

"Fu…fudge. Honestly, it's humiliating, stupid, and not worth all of this drama." First, I shoved my hands in my jeans pockets, but when that didn't feel quite right, I tucked them behind my back. "Can't we just forget about it? We're upsetting the child."

Nobody said anything, everyone still waiting for me to speak. I was not going to get out of this no matter how hard I tried. Dammit. Movements slow and steady, Sam withdrew my arms from behind my back, holding my hands in his larger, warmer ones. He didn't pressure me further. Just held my hands, waiting for me to speak.

"I was walking home late from work last week and the guy ran up to me and grabbed at my bag. He just—he ripped it off my shoulder," I said, doing the best to keep my own voice calm and even. But the frown was definitely back on my face. "But I hung on."

Sam blinked. "You hung on to it?"

"It was Gucci. No way was I just going to let him take it."

Something in the bodyguard's jaw shifted, though nothing was said.

"Anyway, he punched me. Then another couple of guys stepped in to help and I still had a good grip on my bag. Guess he decided it was more trouble than it was worth and took off," I said, blowing out a breath of air. "And they say everyone in New York is rude and unhelpful. Just goes to show."

"Okay." Sam licked his lips in a very distracting manner. Guess I was just in an easily distracted mood. Anything had to be better than thinking about *it* again. "That's everything?"

I nodded.

"Certainly explains why you've been so jumpy."

"I guess it was a bit of a shock. I've never been hit before." My fingers tightened around his and he pulled me closer, gently holding me. Against my ear, his heart beat loud. Odd. I'd never particularly been a cuddler before either. But I suppose everyone had their moments of…not weakness exactly. Something else.

"And you never will be again if I can help it," he said, the words rumbling forth from deep within his solid chest.

"Seriously?" asked Mal. "Is no one going to say the obvious thing here?"

Over on the couch, Dave lifted one shoulder. "It's a bit strange that Martha and Sam are hugging it out, but I guess it's been an emotional day."

"Not that. Man, and you call me the band idiot."

I eased out of Sam's far too nice arms, squaring my shoulders. "Now that's finished, we can all get on with our lives."

Mal clicked his tongue. "Not yet. Also, Davie, what you just said by the way says a lot about you and your need to get over the stuff that went down between you and Marty way back when. Because, dude, we're all way over it. You forgave Jimmy, you can forgive her too."

"I really wish you wouldn't call me that," I mumbled.

"Wish away," said Mal, his expression serious for once. "Now, Marty, sweetie. Listen to me carefully here for a minute. I promise I'll buy you every damn Gucci handbag in the country if the next time someone tries to mug you, you'll just let the bag go. Okay? You hearing me?"

"Thank you," said Ben, still quietly stressing and doing his best to repress his anger over by the wall. I don't think I'd ever actually seen my brother so worked up. At least, not over me. Or not for a very long time. "A handbag is not worth more than your life," he said. "What if the guy had a knife or a gun?"

"Well," I said, searching my mind for a suitably clever response. "He didn't."

"He could have. You're lucky to be alive."

"Ben—"

"Your brother's right," interrupted Sam.

I scowled some more. "I thought you were on my side."

First, the big man tipped his chin, then his hands slowly curled into fists. "Martha, since you don't seem to have noticed, let me point out something important to you. Even when you've done something so breathtakingly stupid that I couldn't figure out what the fuck you could possibly have been thinking, I have still always been on your side."

My mouth, it gaped.

Meanwhile, the silence in the room was deafening. Only for all of about a second, however, until Gibby pulled his thumb out of his mouth and yelled, "Fuck!"

Sam sighed. "Sorry about that, Ben. I'm going to go check on things down at the gate. Excuse me."

Ben just nodded.

More silence. I could feel various people's eyes boring into me. Thankfully, Adam the baby rocker quietly started strumming his guitar. A moment later, Mal joined in with a whisper soft drum beat. "That was weird."

David grunted.

"Of course," said Mal. "It's always weird when unresolved sexual tension boils over like that. Still, gives me something to report back to Anne tonight. We'll have a good gossip about y'all then give making a baby another turn or two. Maybe even three if my wife is lucky. And that girl was born lucky."

Jimmy's lips flattened. "I think it's great that you're planning on starting a family. But I can honestly live without the daily updates regarding your sex life, man."

"But you don't have to, Jimbo. That's the beauty of it, I'm more than happy to share." Mal was clearly quite capable of needling Jimmy even while he accompanied Adam's quiet guitar playing.

Ben slid an arm around my shoulders, his eyes still full of worry.

"You okay? Did you see a doctor or someone when it happened?"

"Oh, I'm fine," I said, a little distracted. "It really is just a black eye. I put some ice on it and then loaded on the concealer. It was fine."

"If you say so. Sorry for raising my voice."

I shrugged. "Guess I should have told you about it."

"You need to learn to be more of a sharer like me, Marty," volunteered Mal. "For instance, you could tell us your plans regarding Sam. To jump his bones or not to jump him, that is the question. Whether 'tis nobler to take the bodyguard to pound town rather than to leave him pining for your hot self indefinitely."

"I had no idea you read Shakespeare."

"I'm cultured. I know shi…stuff," said Mal. "Though we had all agreed after the whole you and Davie hitting the wall thing a decade ago that no one in the family should ever bump uglies again. So you'll be breaking all the rules, you little rebel."

No way was I responding. In fact, every muscle in my body wanted to grab Gibby and get the hell out of the room and away from this excruciating third degree into my history and, apparently, Sam's. But for the life of me I couldn't figure out any way of executing that plan without it looking for all the world like I was running away. Which was exactly what I wanted to do, of course.

I stood my ground and glared at everybody.

After a fair bit of head scratching, David turned his trademarked furrowed brow my way. So much brooding. "How long has that been going on exactly, you and Sam?"

"There's no need to sound like the thought of someone actually being interested in me is so completely unbelievable, David." My hackles were well and truly raised. Men. Such idiots. "Not that it's any of your business."

"Sorry," he grumbled. "Just a surprise. Isn't he like ten years older than you?"

"He's forty-two. Hardly over the hill."

"Yeah, but…he's a really good guy."

"Whereas I'm actual worst of the female race that humanity has to offer?"

"I didn't say that," he said, getting all testy. "Don't put words into my mouth. We just all have a lot of respect for the man. No one wants to see him get hurt."

"You have become a bit of a love 'em and leave 'em, Marty." Mal tutted. "Such a heartbreaker. Don't break Sam's heart, that's all we're saying. No one wants a moping bodyguard. That'd just be plain sad. And possibly dangerous."

"I'll keep that in mind," I said. "Can we talk about something else now?"

"Sam and Martha...huh," said Jimmy, all oblivious like.

Beside me, Ben made a noise of agreement. "Liz told me he was hung up on her a while back."

Apparently not a single one of them understood what something being none of their business meant. I ground my teeth together, trying not to scowl because my face had started to ache. Stupid black eye.

Without missing a beat, Mal flipped back his long blond hair. "You're all incredibly freaking clueless. Sam's around us like twenty-four seven and you don't even notice when shit's going down with him. Because I'm telling you, every time he looks at Marty since about forever, shit is definitely going down with that dude."

"Really?" I asked, despite myself.

"Oh yeah. He gets all tense like his panties are in a wad or something. It's actually quite entertaining."

Fingers moving expertly across the fretboard, Adam changed the music into more of a driving rhythm. "He does watch you a lot."

"See?" asked Mal. "Even young Aaron here has noticed."

"My name's Adam."

"If you say so. Maybe. Though I think you'll find Aaron's an improvement. I'm good at fixing people's names. Just ask Marty."

If looks could kill, Mal would have died under my glare. Probably about fifteen years ago, come to think of it.

On Jimmy's lap, Gibby's eyes were closed, lulled to sleep by the familiar voices and soft strains of music, no doubt. Guess we should have realized Gib had fallen asleep when he failed to repeat Mal's profanity slip. And I'd been trying to talk him into having a nap for hours. Jimmy could out-nanny me without even trying. I actually was the worst.

"I'll carry him up to bed," said Ben, lifting him carefully out of the singer's arms.

Eager to finally escape, I followed, glad to be away from the confusing and complicated array of topics of conversation. Away from the band room, the house was quiet, peaceful. A balm for my frazzled nerves. "Do you really think I could be a manager?"

"I think you could do anything you set your mind to," Ben answered in a similarly low volume. Sweet of him, really. I had no idea his confidence in me ran so high. His big-ass boots padded quietly along the beige carpet. "We're not going to talk about Sam, are we?"

"No."

"Okay, good. Cause he's my employee and you're my sister. Not that I don't care about you both, but if it's all the same to you, I'd rather stay the hell out of it."

"I'd rather you all stayed the hell out of it since it's personal and none of your business." The words came out sharper than I had intended. But the day had not been going according to plan. Maybe if I went back to hiding out in my bedroom at night and keeping Gib away from the practice room during the day, that would work. Me diving behind a couch every time Sam walked in wouldn't be the least bit suspicious. Much. Perhaps facing difficult things didn't fall under my list of specialties. At least, not when it came to one man in particular.

He laughed softly. "C'mon, you know what everyone's like. The chances of them all minding their own business..."

"Great," I said glumly, trudging up the staircase. "Do you think he meant it when he said he was always on my side?"

Ben looked back at me, gaze soft, understanding almost. "Sis, you ever known Sam to say something he didn't mean?"

"No."

"Exactly."

CHAPTER FOUR

"Wat den?"

I exhaled. "Then the train drew a picture."

"Wat den?" asked Gib for about the hundredth time.

"Ah, then the train went for a swim in the pool."

"Wat den?"

"Well, then the train ate his vegetables. All of them. Without any fuss."

"No." His little face scrunched up in disgust. "Wat den?"

"Then the train went to sleep because it was way past his bedtime and he'd been drawing out this whole tell-me-a-story-Aunty-Martha thing for over an hour," I announced. "The end."

"No-no-no!"

"Yes, yes, yes," said Lizzy, wandering over to tuck her son in. "Thank you, Aunty Martha, for the awesome story."

Gib just frowned. He might have gotten that particular facial expression from me, he did it so well. When I leaned down to kiss him on the brow, however, his little hands reached up and clung to my neck for a moment. As if he actually liked me and maybe appreciated the dumb train story. Not that I teared up or anything because how silly.

"Goodnight, sweetheart," I said, giving him an extra kiss.

Gib smothered a yawn. "More twain."

"Tomorrow." Lizzy had her firm-mother voice going on. "That's enough for now. Thank Aunty Martha."

"Tank you," he said tiredly.

"Time to go to sleep," said Liz, delivering her own goodnight kisses. "I love you."

"Mommy..."

"Sweet dreams, baby."

A nightlight turned in slow circles, sending rockets, stars, and hearts moving across the walls. Over in the corner, the toy box was packed full of balls, trucks, a baby bass guitar or two, and various dolls. Gib and I had done a tidy-up earlier and everything seemed in order. Perhaps I wasn't the absolute worst nanny to ever attempt being in charge of a child.

Despite a full evening of playing hide and seek with Lizzy and Gib, a great distraction from the ridiculous conversation in the band room earlier as it turned out, I was wide awake. Then again, it couldn't be any later than around nine. His bedtime might be supposed to be eight, but Gibby turned out to be rather ingenious when it came to extending it until all hours. Especially when his father was over working on songs with Uncle David and unavailable for goodnight kisses. Oh the woe. So much woe. Gib had even managed to squeeze out a couple of fake tears. The child was truly a master manipulator and I couldn't help but be a bit proud of how much effort he put into attempting to get his way. Total dedication to the cause.

"I've never heard of trains going shopping for handbags at Louis Vuitton before," whispered Lizzy, following me out into the hallway, quietly closing the door behind us.

"Every self-respecting train needs a Neverfull."

"Of course they do." She slipped the baby monitor thingy onto her belt. "Can I offer you an alcoholic beverage of some description?"

"Sounds good."

"You know, I was thinking of going for a swim. The pool's heated. Or we could try out the hot tub?"

I nodded. "Good idea. I'm pretty sure he broke at least part of my back making me give him horsey rides today. Meet you down there."

One thing I missed living in New York had been spending quality time at the beach. Not that rooftop pools and bars weren't fun. But they weren't Malibu. That said, Portland wasn't Malibu either, though Ben and Lizzy's outdoor area had been impressively designed and landscaped. During the day, you could see Mount Hood rising in the distance. But night-time was special too. Subdued lighting hid amongst the foliage and under the water, turning it a pale glowing blue. A long glass and stone wall served as an ornate fountain at one end of the pool. Even nature cooperated, delivering up a clear sky with a half moon and scattering of stars high overhead. It was a beautiful night. A peaceful one. And since Ben had gone over to David and Ev's place before Lizzy got home, I could be reasonably certain they hadn't yet had time to confer about today's events. Me managing and Sam's being on my side etcetera. Lizzy would eventually be all over me about it, but not tonight. Thank God.

Meanwhile, Lizzy must have gotten delayed or something. I collected the waiting wine glasses and requisite bottle sitting in ice off an ornate ironwork table. As if we'd be going back and forth from the hot tub.

Funny thing, the hot tub wasn't empty and the person in it definitely wasn't Lizzy.

"Martha," said Sam, raising his head off the edge to appraise my red bikini. "You look nice."

"Thank you." I set the glasses and bottle beside the tub. "Is this a set-up?"

"Not by me."

I frowned on account of it being my go-to expression.

"I'm out here every night after I finish my workout."

"Of course you are." I sighed. "Lizzy would know that."

For a moment he said nothing, his gaze fixed on my face as if he could read me. And he probably could. "Breeze is cool tonight, but the water's good and hot. Are you getting in?"

I nodded and carefully made my way down the steps into the as-promised beautifully warm bubbling water. It did feel dangerously good.

"What's in the bucket?" he asked.

I knelt on the step to inspect the bottle. "Fucking Cristal champagne. This is so a set-up."

"Doesn't say much if you have to be tricked into spending time with me," he said, tone deceptively light.

"You know that's not it."

"Do I? Because I can leave if you like."

With practiced ease, I popped the cork and filled the two glasses, handing him one. "Sam, will you please stay and have a drink with me?"

"Why, Martha, I'd love to." His big hand took the delicate glass from me. Everything about the man was solid, bulky. Not my usual type at all. Next to Sam, I felt positively delicate. Hilarious when you considered how many men I'd scared out of a second date. He made me wish I knew anatomy better. So I could put a name to all of the bumps and bulges in his shoulders and arms. His steamy wet shoulders and arms. "You're staring."

"Hmm?" I asked.

"You're staring at me. Sit down."

"Oh." I sat.

"No need to frown."

"I'm not frowning."

"Whatever you say." His voice was all placid and happy now. I amped my expression up to a scowl. An arm stretched across the edge of the tub, he put the glass to his lips, taking a sip. A wince. "Do you actually like this shit?"

"I don't mind it. Why, what do you drink?"

He took another sip, gaze thoughtful. "Red wine, beer, bourbon if I'm in the mood for liquor."

"The beer and bourbon make sense, but I'd never have picked you as a red wine aficionado."

"No? Nice to know I can still surprise you."

"Oh, you're all about the surprises lately." I stared off into the distance, sipping at the champagne. Between him and the view, the latter would be far less likely to land me in trouble.

"Am I?"

No way was I going there. "Are you aware that answering a question with a question is really annoying?"

"Is it?"

I narrowed my eyes at the man.

But he just laughed. "There, there, Martha. Everything's fine. Relax and drink your champagne."

"Don't tell me what to do," I said, sitting back and taking another sip.

"How did the rest of your day go with Gib?"

"Good, actually. I mean, he half-heartedly kind of threw a couple of peas at me during dinner. But then he asked for me to tell him a bedtime story instead of Liz."

"I said he'd grow to like you. Just needed a little time."

"Yeah, I guess so. Where's your pool housemate, Adam? Off writing another heart-rending ballad about casual sex?"

Sam snorted. "No. Off getting some casual sex, I think. His cell goes off at all hours. I can't keep up."

"Ah to be so young, dumb, and beautiful."

"You know, you're not that much older than him. And while you've made some mistakes, I've never thought you were lacking in smarts," he said. "But you've always been beautiful. You always will be."

"Thank you." I averted my eyes, downed the last of my champagne, and reached for a refill. "That's very kind of you."

"Compliments always did make you squirm."

"Stop it. You don't know everything about me."

"No. But I intend to."

"Why?" My hand jumped as if to punctuate the statement, the cool fizz of champagne sliding over my skin. A pity to waste the good stuff. So I licked it up. There could be no imagining the way his gaze darkened, watching me. Holy cow.

He cleared his throat. "Why what?"

"Why do you want to know everything about me?"

"C'mon, Martha, I only just finished saying you weren't lacking in smarts. Don't prove me wrong."

I huddled into my corner of the hot tub, clutching at my drink. Not feeling defensive, just…all right, so I was feeling defensive. "Maybe I just want to hear you say it. Everyone else seems to have a damn opinion about us. Who knew rock stars were such damn gossips? Sticking their collective noses in everybody else's business all the time."

"They care about you, that's all." Sam placed his glass on the side and stood, moving over to sit beside me. Very close beside me. Our knees were even touching, all intimate-like. Then his gentle fingers turned my chin, making me face him. "Let me see."

"What?" Ever so carefully, he wiped away the worst of my concealer and makeup from beneath my right eye. His calluses slid across my skin in a not un-nice manner. "Yuck. Don't. It's ugly."

"Just let me see."

"Maybe I should have worn big sunglasses around all of the time and told everyone I was permanently hungover. They probably would have believed it."

"Then you'd have had Jimmy dragging you off to rehab and

offering to be your sponsor."

"True." I grimaced. "You were the only one in there today who wasn't angry at me."

"About holding on to the bag instead of letting the robber take it?"

"Yes."

He half-smiled. "Martha, my dear, I was fucking furious. But it was neither the time nor place to get into it with all of the guys gathered around."

"What do you mean?"

"What I mean is…if you were mine, I'd have turned your ass bright pink for what you did," he said, all scarily matter of fact. "Thinking a handbag was more important than your life."

My eyes opened wide in surprise.

"What kind of ridiculous shit is that?"

"Guess I'm not as smart as you thought I was."

"No. You just don't know how loved you are," he corrected, his thumb stroking across my cheek. The man touched me like I was precious. But also like he already owned me and for some reason I didn't have it in me to disagree. "For a woman with so much pride, Martha, you have a very thin grasp of your own worth."

I didn't know what to say to that. Yet what with his hands suddenly grasping my waist and lifting me onto his lap, any attempt at coherency on my part fled the tub completely. Since when exactly did we start sitting on one another?

"At any rate, you and I are going to start doing some self-defense work together," he announced. "Should anything like it happen again in future, you'll know how to react. Regardless of what fucking designer handbag you're carrying."

"Are you giving me orders?"

"Do you disagree with the idea?"

"Well, no. But you could have asked instead of phrasing it the way you did."

"I'll make a note of that for next time. Now," he said. "I believe you wanted some sort of statement from me as to my intentions."

"Your intentions?"

Sam lifted the bottle of champagne out of the bucket of ice and topped up my glass. Next his arms wrapped tight around me before any kind of escape could be attempted. The man knew exactly what he was doing. But if ever a man was bound to have a plan, it would be him. "Have a bit more to drink. It'll make you feel better."

"I'm fine. Or I was fine where I was. What am I doing sitting on your lap?"

"You never did like being out of control of a situation."

"Stop acting as if you know what's going on in my head all the time. You don't!"

He chuckled, the sound and the vibration of his strong chest against my side much too pleasant. "Considering I've been waiting for you for almost a decade, I think I've got a pretty good understanding of what goes in that gorgeous head of yours."

"Almost a decade?"

"Mm-hmm." He took a drink from my glass, wrinkling his nose at the taste. "No, I definitely don't think that champagne's going to grow on me anytime soon. Anyway, where was I?"

"Almost a decade…"

"Right. So—"

"That's not possible."

"Of course it is."

I shook my head. No one had ever wanted me for anywhere near so long. David and I had barely lasted half that amount of time before outgrowing each other and breaking up in a spectacularly messed-up fashion. Though mostly, he'd outgrown me. Left me far behind and largely forgotten. Or at least that's the way it felt at the time. Since then, I'd dated men for a month or two at most. Then dumped them before they could dump me because better safe than sorry and hurt. Yet with Sam came a strange sense of safety. He provided exactly the sort of shelter I'd fled New York in search of, if I was being totally honest. The comfort of loved ones, family, and maybe even friends. Things I hadn't had for a long time. Things I hadn't quite been able to provide for myself, irritatingly enough. But to maybe need someone, to actually make myself vulnerable…

"This doesn't make sense," I said in a quiet voice.

"No?"

I shook my head and sipped my champagne. It didn't make me feel any better. So there, he didn't know everything. "So if this thing is a decade old, then why are we here now? After all this time?"

"You've always been a loner. Self-contained."

"True."

"But, I don't know. It just seems like there's something different about you, ever since you've been back," he said. "Never struck me before that you weren't happy with your life, and how it was going…"

"Yes, but ten years?"

"You're really stuck on that, aren't you? Let me explain," he said, taking a deep breath. "You see, when I first started to work with the boys, I was all about the job. A lot of people think that's the only way to do what I do. Total commitment. Seven days a week around the clock. Don't even think of having a life of your own, let alone a relationship. Which was fine in my thirties. You were still wound up over Davie and needed time to get yourself sorted. So I put it off. Told myself it was the right thing to do."

"Wouldn't getting involved with me when I was working for them too have been a conflict of interest or something?"

He lifted one big shoulder. "Possibly. But I'm pretty sure we could have worked it out."

"Huh."

"Then you up and left, moved to New York. That was a bit of a shock, honestly."

"Was it?"

"Yeah. Though you still came back now and then. Plus there'd be shows on the East Coast and you'd usually turn up," he said. "Thing was, when you were around, you were still angry. All pissed off about David and Ev getting together and being all happy and in love. So obviously, it still wasn't the right time. But that's okay. When it came to you, I was used to being patient."

I drank my champagne. David had pretty much written a whole album dedicated to how much I sucked. While we'd both had our faults, I couldn't exactly say he was wrong. So the less my ex got mentioned the better.

Sam smiled. "Now, however, things feel different."

"In what way?"

"Well, these days when you see Dave, you mostly just seem awkward and a bit embarrassed about the whole thing."

My spine snapped straight. "No, I don't."

"No? Okay. So I'm wrong."

"You don't really believe that. You're just trying to pacify me."

"Here's what I believe…" He took another drink from my glass. "Martha, dearest, I'm not going to argue with you about shit that doesn't matter."

I just blinked.

"If you say you're not worried about being around Dave, then great. I'm delighted to hear it," he said. "All I care about is that you're obviously no longer hung up on the guy."

"Of course I'm not."

"And then there's the other thing."

"What other thing?"

"The part where you haven't screeched at me to let you go or even attempted to climb off my lap since I put you there a good…oh, I'd say four or five minutes ago now."

I froze.

"Rather important, don't you think?"

"I did think about it."

"Screeching or escaping?" he asked calmly.

"Escaping."

"But you didn't." He pressed a soft damp kiss to my forehead. "Very brave of you, Martha."

"Why do I always feel like a child throwing a tantrum around you?"

"I definitely don't think of you as a child."

"Yes, I'm aware of that. Your huge hard-on is sticking into my hip."

"Like I said, I've been waiting a long time. Just ignore it. God knows, I'm trying to," he said. "As for the other, you do enjoy a good tantrum from time to time. But I rather enjoy your sharp edges. Keeps me on my toes."

I finished the champagne and held the glass out for a refill.

"You have tomorrow off, don't you?" he asked, pouring the bottle with precision. "Because you're going to have a headache in the morning if you keep drinking."

I chugged the champagne like a lady. "Fill it again."

"I am your servant in all things."

"Bullshit."

"You'd be bored out of your beautiful brains in under two minutes if I was the sort of man you could walk all over." He chuckled. "Maybe less wriggling around on my dick unless you'd like to up the timeline for things happening between us. I'm amenable. It's up to you really. Just a polite warning."

I froze. "Hold up. The timeline?"

"Hmm?"

"Did you actually just say there was a timeline?"

"What?" he asked, seemingly perplexed.

"Fucking oversized ex-Navy SEAL alpha jerk control freak," I grumbled. "You have, haven't you? You've actually planned out to the day exactly how you think things are going to go down between us?"

At this, the man seemed to hesitate for once. Wise of him really. "I wouldn't dare assume when it came to you, my love."

"Oh, you liar. Let me guess, first a date. Somewhere nice, an intimate evening at a good restaurant." I tapped a fingernail against my lips. "A few romantic moves, some hand-holding and deep and meaningful looks over dinner maybe. Then bang! Sex."

"Ah, well…"

"I mean, you might have ideally wanted to wait until date two or three before taking things into the bedroom. But you have been waiting almost a decade as the boner sticking into my side keeps reminding me. So yes, we'll fuck after the first date." I saluted him with my glass of champagne before downing some more. My throat was so dry and my adrenaline levels high. It couldn't be more necessary. "Around about that time, you'll have a word with the guys to make sure they're all aware that you and I are together and everyone's fine with it. Because you're all such a well-honed pack of male idiots who've been running together for so long."

He just looked at me. The man had an excellent poker face. But I could tell…

"Yes, you'll probably go out for a beer with my brother to start the whole advanced male bonding becoming a family one day thing. After that, you'll want us to starting thinking about moving in together, getting our own place," I said. Because that's exactly what everyone else would do. And it might have been nice to be like everyone else, but I'd never quite fit no matter how hard I tried. Attempting normal would inevitably end in ruin. "Then, give it…oh say three months, we'll go on vacation somewhere nice like Hawaii and you'll pop the question. You've already saved up for the ring, haven't you? Probably even got one picked out somewhere. Admit it, you do, don't you?"

His lips stayed firmly shut.

"I'm not the only one who's been paying attention, Sam," I said. "Get you started and you're like a robot with a stick up its ass with all of the organizing and planning everything. But I'm neither your job nor a combat mission, buddy."

"Can you put a stick up a robot's ass? I guess it depends on the type of robot really, doesn't it?"

"Shut up. You know what I mean."

"So you don't like Hawaii then?" he asked mildly.

"I don't like being managed."

"I see."

"If we're doing this—" I said, setting my glass aside and wriggling my way off his lap. Because I would wriggle if I damn well wanted to. His arms reluctantly let me go, his gaze tense and watchful. "—and that is a definite *if*—then I'm in charge."

"You're in charge," he repeated rather more slowly.

"Is that going to be a problem?"

He paused. "Absolutely not."

"That's the correct answer."

Serve him right if I left him hanging. Mind you, it seemed a shame to waste such a magnificent hard-on. Also, when it came to making skin to skin contact with the man, I apparently had pressing needs. Seriously urgent ones. And since physical needs were far easier than emotional to deal with, I climbed back onto his lap, straddling him this time. He immediately gripped my waist, holding me steady all protective-like. My hands meanwhile smoothed over his very lovely shoulders. A hungry gaze slid over me, making my pussy tingle. We'd barely gotten started and he had me all worked up. Without a doubt, the man had skills. Always nice to know up front that you weren't wasting your time.

"No more of this timeline nonsense either," I said, sounding a bit more breathy than I would have liked.

"You're on top. Understood."

"Good." I nodded, grinding against him. Christ. Everything low in me tightened with need, it felt so fucking amazing. Horny was far safer than attempting to deal with heart stuff. "I'm using you for sex and that's all that's happening between us right now."

His brows rose. "You're using me for sex?"

"Yes."

"Huh."

"Is that all you have to say?" I asked.

"Well...always happy to be of service. Whenever you're ready."

Nails digging into the back of his neck just a little, I cocked my head. "Is that a dare I'm hearing, Sam?"

"Martha, my love." His smile, it was pure predator. "You bet it is."

CHAPTER FIVE

Never one to be outdone, I shoved my hand down the front of his board shorts and grabbed his cock. Hot skin and hard flesh more than filled my hand. All the while, his hooded gaze stayed glued to my face, doing his best to read me no doubt. But I was in charge. Not him. And pushing aside my bikini bottoms and sinking down on him more than demonstrated that fact.

"M-Martha," he stammered, fingers digging into my hips almost hard enough to bruise. His eyelids slammed shut. "Fuck."

The man was large. Thicker than I'd expected. Some wriggling was definitely required. I panted, gripping his neck tightly, my cheek pressed against his. Bit by bit, I took all of him inside me. An adjustment period would also be needed. Holy hell. "Just give me a moment."

"Give you a moment?" He shifted his hold, strong arms surrounding me. "I think you just killed me."

"What? Why?"

"It didn't occur to you to give me any warning?"

"Me grabbing your penis didn't signal something was about to happen?"

His laughter came from deep inside his chest, brutally low and rough. Hands stroked firmly down my spine, soothing me. There may or may not have been an air of possession about the way he touched me. I don't know. Other things were on my mind right then. Like figuring out how to breathe and keep my heart beating with his big dick inside of me. "Guess I should have asked about protection etcetera."

"That might have been wise." More laughter. "I'm clean. Tested regularly."

"Yes, same, regularly. I always have, promise."

"I know. Wouldn't have let you grab my dick without a lengthy discussion otherwise."

"Then what the hell were you complaining about just now?" I rested my chin on his shoulder, getting comfortable. For such a hard man, he was awfully comfy. "Honestly, Sam. Talk about mixed signals."

"Most women like a little foreplay first is all."

"Oh, that."

"We haven't even kissed." His mouth moved up my neck, hot and seductive. Teeth nipped and his tongue dragged over my skin, lighting up every single freaking nerve in me. "Not that I'm complaining."

"Do that again."

He obliged as I rocked my hips, rising and falling just a little. There was no rush. And testing his stamina appealed to me. Fingers tugged at the ties on my bikini top, loosening the straps. Soon I was as bare chested as him, my stiff nipples brushing against his hard pecs and smattering of chest hair. Interesting to note that sensation wise, chest hair had been much underrated. Most of the guys I'd screwed previously had shaved or waxed. But this was much nicer.

One hand palmed a breast, the other holding the back of my neck. All the better to guide my mouth to his. It wasn't a polite first kiss. But then, I guess we were probably well past that stage. His firm lips pressed hard against mine, slick tongue sliding into my mouth. The man kissed me with a decade's worth of hunger and longing. I might not have known for quite that long, but I answered him just the same. We owned each other. Mouths fused and hands grasping.

Finished with kneading my breast, he traced down to where we were joined. The pad of his thumb rubbed around my clit, tantalizing me and making everything that much more urgent.

"That's it," he murmured.

I rode him harder, taking his thick girth. With him working me, dragging things out this time wasn't an option. Someone had obviously given the man a map to my body. Or he simply was that good. Either way, my pussy tightened on him. Everything in me drawing impossibly tight before boom! Orgasmic explosion. It was the big bang all over again. I came harder than I had possibly ever. My body shaking, every muscle trembling. All of the good hormones rushed through me, sending me sky high.

"Christ." Gripping my hips tight, he slammed me down on him over and over. Until finally he came too. "Martha."

If I hadn't been busy biting his shoulder I might have answered. Doubtful though. My mind had been wiped clean, every part of me floating and yet weirdly heavy with lassitude. It was entirely possible I'd never come down. His body shook, pelvis grinding against me. We were plastered together, not a hairsbreadth of space between us. My arms were wrapped tight around his neck. Possibly suffocating him. But honestly, such were the risks of making a woman come that hard.

And so easily. Damn.

Next time I'd make him work harder for it. Try out a couple of different positions and really put him to the test. Yes, good call. Using Sam for sex might just be the best idea I'd ever had. Or possibly the worst, given how scarily addictive sex with him could become. Maybe I should take a breath before already mentally planning our next encounter.

"What are you thinking about?" he asked, clever fingers massaging my back, rubbing my neck.

"Nothing," I lied. "You didn't even think to ask if I was on contraception."

He shrugged. "A baby would be fine. After all, I'm not getting any younger."

"You did not just say that." I sat up, aghast. It took a moment to untangle ourselves and another to find my bikini top. "A baby…fucking hell, Sam."

"Too much?" His smile was small but sneaky. Very sneaky. "I think you'd make a wonderful mother. Look how good you are with Gib."

"I'm on contraception, thank you very much."

"Of course you are. It was just a thought. But on the timeline it was still a year or so down the track."

Given how much effort I put into glaring at the man, his magnanimous expression was irritating as all hell. While he tucked himself back into his pants, I concentrated on righting my bikini. Because it would be wonderful if anyone looking out the windows saw me half naked. Absolutely wonderful. Maybe semi-public sex in my brother's hot tub hadn't been the best idea. Especially since it had started Sam talking about children, of all things. Though the orgasm really had been something.

"Relax, Martha," he said. "I'm just joking. Of course you're not ready to discuss children *yet*."

My mouth really did gape this time. "I said I was just using you for sex."

"And you did."

"That's all. Just sex."

"All right then."

He put his hands behind his head, all relaxed-like. Not getting distracted by the way the position made his muscles bulge was harder than it should have been. Especially given how angry he'd made me. Thank God for champagne. I grabbed another glassful, sitting safely opposite and well away from him. If ever a man seemed to delight in pressing my buttons. Though he didn't just press them. He jabbed at those bastards for all he was worth and then sat back and clapped when I went off. Asshole. And they said age brought you wisdom. Boy were they wrong.

"You are such a shit stirrer," I grumbled.

"Sorry, love."

"Stop calling me that," I said. "And if you ever repeat that crap about us having children I am never fucking you ever again."

"That would be sad. I thought for a first time we didn't do too badly."

Silence descended. Stars twinkled. I sipped my champagne and tried to re-find my post-orgasmic bliss. "You think you can do better?"

"I know so."

"Hmm."

He waded across the tub, stopping when my outstretched hand hit his chest. "I'm not allowed to show you affection after sex?"

"A. I like my space. B. You've pissed me off."

Instead of retreating, however, he stayed put, stroking my hand and toying with my fingers. The same ones holding him back. Such a ridiculous man, behaving as if we were suddenly a couple or something. Either that or a very determined one.

His gaze when he looked at me was gentle, far too warm. "Like I said, I've been waiting for you for a long time. I was a little worked up. Next time will be much better, I promise."

Much better might kill me. Still, it was an intriguing idea. "I'll give it some thought."

"You do that."

"I'm going up to bed now. Alone." And while climbing over the edge of an inbuilt hot tub in a bikini might not be the most elegant exit, it was, however, certainly the most expedient. With the overly demonstrative mood Sam was in, he'd probably want to hug or something, which would be misleading for everyone involved. That wasn't what we were. Whatever exactly we were.

"Night, love," he said cheerfully. Apparently undeterred.

"Stop calling me that," I hissed, collecting the remnants of the bottle of Cristal on my way. Be a pity to waste it and I was in need of something to calm me down.

Behind me, he chuckled, all amused. The jerk. In a display of great maturity and grace, I ignored him and got the hell out of there. I had the worst feeling I might not in fact be winning when it came to our verbal sparring. Perhaps all of the information, emotions, and sex had boggled my brain. Tomorrow I'd have a better handle on things. A clearer perspective.

Inside the house, Lizzy was wisely nowhere in sight. A second bottle of Cristal waited on my bedside table along with some candles for mood lighting. She probably thought she'd been setting up quite the lovenest for Sam and me. As if. I'd catch up with her later, the conniving girl.

And I did not lie awake for hours frowning at the ceiling thinking about him. That would just be stupid. For some reason, however, sleep didn't come. But surely it had nothing to do with him. Because whatever Sam's original plans might have been, we were just using each for sex. Therefore, there could be no possible reason for me to be freaking out about all of his relationship talk. Sex. Nothing more. Nothing less. Just really great sex. Apparently, even better than what we'd had tonight and it had been rather fucking great. Though he might have just been bragging. Though as my brother had said, Sam wasn't the type to say something he didn't mean.

Hmm.

Since I couldn't sleep, I drank some more champagne, because why not? That's unfortunately when the bad thing happened.

"Heard someone was seen skulking out of the pool house this

morning in the early hours." The drummer grinned. Most likely the housekeeper had ratted me out. For some reason she thought Mal was delightful. "Fast work, Marty. You go, girl."

Jimmy just seemed amused at the news. But David and Ben gave me startled glances. Hypocrites. As if neither of them had copulated in the history of space and time. My brother had even rather infamously impregnated Mal's then twenty-one-year-old sister-in-law. It had caused all sorts of trouble within the band and their entourage. Sam and I getting it on barely rated as news compared to that scandal.

With three children under the age of three running around, telling the man to go fuck himself was out of the question. Sadly. Still, my smile was all sharp teeth. "Why, thank you, Malcolm. You know how I value your input into these things."

Gibby, along with Jimmy and Lena's twin girls, were building and destroying towers of blocks faster than I could keep track. The creative and destructive power of small children was awe-inspiring. Also the range of floor space they managed to spread their toys across. I sat on the ground nearby, doing my best to try to keep it contained to one general corner of the room. But alas, I was no match for their sheer exuberance. Blocks were everywhere.

Since the band had been putting the finishing touches to some new songs, everyone was in attendance. Even Adam had been running around, acting as both errand boy and roadie. He tuned guitars and fetched things, all while avoiding my gaze whenever possible. Suited me fine. The less said about last night the better. At least Sam had been busy organizing security for a show next week for charity and hadn't yet made an appearance.

But of course, Mal wasn't even remotely finished. "Poor Adam. Did you get any sleep at all, man? How thin are the walls out there in the pool house of love?"

Adam just gave me a worried look. "I didn't say anything."

Oh, God.

"You didn't say anything about what exactly?" asked Mal, twirling a drumstick in one hand. "Not holding out on us are you, dude?"

The kid froze.

"Can't hold out on your fellow band members. That's not cool."

His brows drew in. "I'm a solo act."

"Yeah," said Mal. "But I'm playing on your album under my

awesome new secret name, Sticks McGee. Ingenious, right?"

"That's the stupidest thing I've ever heard." Ben didn't even bother to look up from where he was busily making notes on a pad of paper. "You're playing uncredited like we decided. I don't want any of the attention taken away from Adam. It's his debut album."

"Fine, whatever. But he still has to tell us what he knows." Given they were both around the same height, Mal couldn't quite loom over the kid. But he certainly tried. Peer pressure at its finest. "Is Marty a screamer? Likes to make farm animal noises in bed? Or no, did she say mean things during sex and make Sam cry? C'mon, what went down? You can tell me."

My hands bunched into fists. "Mal..."

"What? No," stammered Adam. "She just...I mean, it's not even a big deal and...it was just an accident."

"Not another word." Normally, violence wasn't my thing. But I might punch someone. "I mean it."

Ben just shook his head.

David looked vaguely confused.

Jimmy, meanwhile, was now wearing quite a broad smile. "What did you do?"

"Nothing," I lied with much vehemence. "Nothing happened!"

"Adam, my boy." Mal continued to twirl the stick in a vaguely threatening manner. "Don't make me use the drumsticks of death on you. It's not a nice way to go."

The children laughed and clapped at the idiot drummer's display. Like he needed any encouragement. But Adam's gaze kept darting between me and Mal, trying to decide whose wrath would be mightier and scarier. And since Mal stood closer, I lost.

"She just got the room wrong, is all," Adam blurted out, finally. "Thought mine was Sam's and stumbled in a little drunk."

I hung my head and covered my face. So I missed seeing Sam stride into the room, assessing the situation in an instant. Or perhaps our voices had carried.

Mal's hyena cackle filled the big room. "Oh. My. God. You poor young innocent thing to have to face down Marty's lusts all alone in the dark like that. Were you terrified? I know I would have been. Tell me more."

Sam sighed, crouching down behind me. What should have been a comfort was not on account of how he actually fucking told them. "Then she slapped him on the ass and declared it was booty call time. Fortunately I had, however, heard her enter the building and intervened."

"What'd you do, Sam? What'd you do?"

"I threw the slightly intoxicated lady in question over my shoulder and told young Adam to go back to sleep since I'd be dealing with the situation," said Sam, who I now officially hated. Unfortunately, ex-Navy SEAL. So when I tried to jab him with my elbow, he simply caught it and gave me a smile. "Sorry, love. But I'm afraid that story was always going to get out. Especially once Adam opened his mouth and Malcolm caught wind of it. Best that they hear about it now, have their laugh, and then get on with their lives."

"How could you?" I growled.

"It's going to be all right."

"They're never going to let me live this down."

My brother shook his head, mumbling something about neither wanting nor needing to know about my sex life. I hadn't wanted him, or any of the others, to know either. And I couldn't even bring myself to see what expression David had on his face. But while Jimmy had the manners to at least turn his head away to chuckle, Mal was outright crying from laughing so hard. "We really aren't. We're going to give you shit about this forever and ever."

"No, you're not," said Sam simply. "Because if you do, I'll accidentally hurt you sometime when you least expect it."

"Y-you'll hurt me?"

"Yes."

"Are we talking really bad like blood and stuff?" asked Mal. "Or just a little bad like a stubbed toe or something? Because that would probably be worth it."

"The first one."

At this, Mal's joy up and disappeared. "Good God, that's harsh. Also, I don't see how you can do it accidentally."

"Never you mind. I'll find a way."

"It'll never work. We're totally untouchable. We're protected by this kick-ass bodyguard. You know the guy I mean. What's his name again? Help me out here."

"You pay me to protect you from other people," growled the

bodyguard. "Not from myself. And I don't like anyone upsetting my woman, is that understood?"

My shoulders stiffened at his words.

"Right then, so this is never to be mentioned again." Sam set a hand on my shoulder, rubbing lightly. "We all make mistakes. Time to move on."

"Well, this isn't cool. I don't think I like you and Marty getting together after all," said Mal, the edges of his lips turned sadly downwards. "I'm still telling Anne all about what happened last night and you can't stop me because it's hilarious. After that, I guess I'll let it go. But only because I'm a wonderful caring human being and not because you threatened me with bodily harm."

"Thank you, Malcolm. Knew we could rely on your discretion."

There was multiple clearing of throats and eventually they got busy doing their own thing again. Sam, however, stayed crouched at my side. "You have marker on you."

"Gib decided he wanted to draw on me," I said. "Give me tattoos like his father and friends."

Sam leaned in, inspecting the artwork. "An interesting idea. Though your face was pretty enough without whatever that's meant to be."

"It's a tractor, apparently. I can't believe you told them." Hands rubbed at my shoulders, trying to soothe. And failing miserably. "Anyone could have made that mistake. I wasn't even very drunk. It was just really dark and I didn't want to turn on the lights and wake anyone up. How was I to know it was the wrong ass I was slapping?"

Sam nodded in sympathy. If there was some sign of amusement in his eyes, I chose to ignore it. This time, at least.

"This thing between us was supposed to be secret," I said. "Private."

"Have you ever known anything that happened around this bunch and managed to remain private?"

I just scowled.

Music started up and children played and my mind was a fucking mess. But Sam waited, as patient as ever. Whatever we were, this wasn't the place to discuss it. Not that I particularly ever wanted to discuss the situation between us. After all, nothing wrong with being fuck buddies.

"You're not ashamed of me, are you?" he asked.

"No," I said, mildly outraged. "That's not it at all. I just...and you called me your woman. What was that about?"

"Oh, I was just using terms they'd understand to make sure they didn't give you any crap." He waved the words away like they were little more than a pesky bug. "No big deal."

Only it kind of was. Yet there'd been enough drama today without me going off. Me being the center of attention here was not what I wanted, contrary to popular opinion. My particular brand of bitch might be all about me getting my way. But it wasn't all about me getting my way with every damn person watching. A fine yet important distinction in my life.

At least Gibby and the twins had been too busy playing to pay attention and learn any new and fascinatingly inappropriate words. One small relief.

"Don't frown, love. Everything's fine."

With a sigh, I chilled, easing up on whatever pissy expression I'd been wearing. I couldn't even particularly be bothered getting angry with him about the endearment, though I did manage a mumbled "Stop calling me that."

"Sorry."

I took a deep breath. "And I'm not ashamed of you. I would never be ashamed of you. That's a ridiculous idea."

"Holy hell," said Mal, breaking off from the song with a clatter of percussion, and pointing at us with a drum stick. "Did you guys see that? It's like he's the Martha Whisperer. Could have sworn she was going to go off and he just totally talked her down. Not even you used to be able to do that, Davie."

"Malcolm," said Sam sternly.

"Sorry, sorry. I'm totally minding my own business."

"That'll be the day," said Ben. "Can we get back to work now?"

Sam planted a kiss on top of my head. In front of everyone. I could feel curious eyes on us. But they could all be ignored. Talk about a situation getting out of hand. And it hadn't even been twenty-four hours since we'd had our pseudo relationship whatever discussion. Things were happening too fast. All I'd wanted was to crawl all over him and use him as my very own personal sex toy. God, talk about complicated. Maybe we should slow things down.

"We're fine, right?" I asked. "I mean, we're still friends?"

"Of course we are. You even know which bedroom's mine now

when you're feeling in the mood." His thumb brushed over Gib's artwork. Then he gave my fading black eye a quick grimace. "I've got to get back to work. Will I see you later?"

Ziggy came in then and called him away on some business. Just as well. I didn't have an answer.

CHAPTER SIX

The first problem with Sam was that every time I got even close to pondering the possibility of there perhaps being an "us," he did something to freak me out. The second was how he refused to play by the rules. My rules.

"We agreed I'd be in charge. But I don't feel like I'm in charge," I panted, hitting the boxing bag thingy with my carefully wrapped hands. Liz and Ben had taken Gib out to see the latest kid's movie. Even Adam had taken himself out for the night. We had the house to ourselves and Sam had decided we should spend our time in the gym. "If I chip a nail, I will not be happy."

Standing behind the bag, Sam held it steady. "Your nails will be fine. Wouldn't make much sense you being in charge during your self-defense classes though, would it?"

"'spose not."

"Don't pout. You can be in charge after."

"I'm not pouting." I half-heartedly flung my fists in a one-two type motion at the bag. "Will this be the same as when I was supposedly in charge, yet you dragged me out of my room to come do this?"

"I didn't drag you out of your room. After all, it's not like you were in there hiding from me, is it?"

"No," I lied. "My arms are tired. My shoulders hurt too."

"You've done very well." He smiled, turning me around so he could massage my back. Something he was exceptionally good at. "What are the three attack points again?"

"Eyes, throat, and groin."

"And what do you do with the handbag?"

"Let the mugger take it without a fight."

"Good girl."

With my back to him, he couldn't see my scowl. "It wasn't that I valued the handbag more than my life, you know. It's just that it was mine. You have to fight to protect what's yours in this world, or people will walk all over you."

"Fair point." Followed with silence.

"But?"

More silence. Then, "You ever read anything by Miyamoto Musashi?"

"Should I have?"

"Seventeenth century warrior poet. Samurai."

"Oh, *that* Miyamoto Musashi. Sure, of course. I have his collected works upstairs in my suitcase."

He ignored my sarcasm, and continued on with the massage. And, apparently, the history lesson. "There's some debate about whether Musashi was the greatest swordsman of all time. But what nobody questions was his judgment. He studied his rivals for years, only challenging them when he was good and ready, and never letting his ambition cloud his choice. Because one wrong decision of opponent or timing and he would die."

"There's a lesson here, I just know it."

"If one of the greatest warriors of all time needed to learn to pick his fights, then maybe you can too."

I sighed. "Okay. Message received." His thumbs dug into something particularly needy in my neck and I groaned in bliss. "Why couldn't you have done this last night in the pool house?"

"Because you were drunk and needed to sleep it off."

"That's what irritates me the most about Adam opening his big mouth and telling them. It's not even like anything happened afterwards," I said. "There's a reason why they call it a booty call instead of a spooning call, Sam."

He chuckled, talented fingers moving down one of my arms, working the sore muscles. Of course, this necessitated him fitting his front to my back. Goosebumps raced up and down my spine at his nearness. If only his body against mine didn't feel so good. Made holding out against him nearly impossible.

"Where's all this tension coming from?" he asked, rubbing at my wrist before moving onto the palm of my hand, undoing the tape as he went. "Have a rough day, my love?"

"You're going to insist on calling me that no matter how many times I ask you not to, aren't you?"

"Sorry. It just slips out. Does it really bother you?"

I shrugged, unwilling or unable to answer. I didn't know. His slick mouth teased my neck while he massaged my fingers before moving on to the other arm. Teeth nibbled at the sensitive lobes of my ear. It made me all tingly. "I'm sweaty."

"I like you sweaty," he said, voice lower than usual. The man was definitely turned on, as the hardening cock against my butt signalled. Made it impossible not to press back against him. His arm muscles flexed, holding me tighter while keeping up with the massage. No doubts regarding Sam's ability to multi-task. "Sorry for holding out on you last night."

"You and your annoying morals. Though it probably was the right thing to do given how drunk I was." I sighed, reaching back to stroke my fingers over the stubble on the back of his shaved head. The thick muscles of his neck. Every chance I did some grabbing and kneading of my own. Honestly, my own body's reaction to him was crazy. Already, my core ached with need as if I hadn't had sex in ages.

"Still," I said. "Maybe I should hold out on you just the same."

"You don't really want to do that, love." His voice sounded far too confident. "We have far too much fun together when we play nicely."

"Maybe."

"Definitely. I like your sports bra."

"It's nothing special."

"Maybe not," he said. "But the woman in it is."

"Smooth line, Sam. I'm impressed. Is there a lock on that door?"

"Brilliant minds think alike. I locked it when we came in." He kissed a line down the side of my neck, his hand slipping beneath the waistband of my shorts. While his fingers might have been thick, they certainly were dexterous. First he cupped my mound, petting those lips lightly. "You have such a sweet cunt, love. How lucky am I to be the man who gets to play with it?"

I smiled. "Sweet? How would you know? You've never even tasted it."

"Now that's a very good point."

Strong arms lifted me, laying me on a bench press or whatever you call those things. My shorts and underwear were whisked down my legs. Only sneakers are kind of a pain in the ass to get clothes over. So they needed to go too. With an impatient growly noise, Sam dealt with them and the socks, and then the clothes. All of it was thrown haphazardly over his shoulder. I'd never seen a man in such a hurry to get at me. In the end, all I still wore was the bra. He knelt at the end of the bench, parted my legs with his hands, and stopped.

Just fucking stopped.

"What are you doing?" I asked, craning my neck to see.

"I don't want to rush this."

"Well, I do."

"Shh, relax." Hands stroked the outside of my thighs, placing my legs gently over his big shoulders. And all the while, he stared at my vagina like he was transfixed or something. "You're so beautiful, Martha. Every part of you. I want you to feel cherished."

Huh. "Thank you."

He kissed the inside of my thigh. Yet went no closer.

"Can you take a photo with your cell later and cherish that instead?"

"What a lovely idea. I'll do that too."

I groaned. "Sam…"

With a quick grin, he dipped his head and licked up my center. Christ. My back bowed, eyelids fluttering closed. I'd already been wet when he started touching me. Now I was drenched. Fingers dug into my flesh, holding my legs apart for him to feed. Because the man ate me like he was starving. There could be no other description. Some guys just gave you a lick or two then moved on to the fucking segment of the evening as if they'd ticked the good guy head box and had earned their reward. But not so with Sam. He licked and stroked and generally drove me out of my mind. If his whole upper body wound up covered in my juices, I wouldn't have been the least bit surprised.

The man obviously loved going down on a woman.

Well, this woman, at least.

His tongue dragged, dug, circled, and swirled over and around the pertinent parts of my anatomy. As if he needed to learn me inside and out for some later test. Without a doubt, he'd have passed with flying colors. The first orgasm hit me hard and had me shaking from top to toe. The second swept through me like a wave of ecstasy. Forget massages for total body and muscle relaxation. Unless they were massages done by Sam's tongue to my pussy. Sign me up for one of those suckers any day.

"And you're especially beautiful," he said with a smile, wiping off his face with a hand, "right after you've come."

I lay on the bench, still twitching, watching as he took off his shirt and shorts. Such a sight to see. The rock-hard length of his cock pointed straight at the ceiling. And I wanted it, I really did. But there was just one small problem. "I'm not sure I can move."

"Let me help." He lifted me off the bench so carefully, wrapping my legs around him seemed only polite. "Is the wall all right with you? The bench is the wrong height and the flooring's a bit rough in here. Wouldn't want you to get carpet burn on your soft skin."

"The wall is fine."

"Excellent."

With my spine pressed to the cool flat surface, he reached between us, positioning the broad, blunt head of his cock at my entrance. There was less wriggling this time on account of me being so wet. In he pushed, slowly lowering me onto him. God, the feeling of fullness, the stretch of him inside me. Twenty-four hours was far too long to go without. I pressed my lips against his, kissing him deep and hungry. No need for messing around. No worrying about if he wanted me plastered all sweaty against his skin.

Sam knew me and wanted me. How much was honestly a little scary.

Hips flexing, he fucked himself into me time and again. Each measured perfect thrust stealing my breath and blowing my mind. His fingers tightened on my ass, digging in to hold me in place. The man steadily nailed me to the damn wall. Only he kept subtly, slightly shifting his position, searching for something. I didn't realize what until he hit something inside my pussy that made my whole body clench.

"There we go," he said.

"Christ. That's why they call them drill sergeants, huh?"

"Don't be silly." He grinned. "That's the army, love. I'm navy."

Then he set about fucking me into oblivion. Over and over, he hit that one perfect place, sending me higher with each stroke. I clung to him, struggling for breath, body and heart turned inside out. As for my mind, it was total mush. Faster and harder, he fucked me against the wall, hammering my g-spot. Not stopping until I came again, shouting out a name. Someone's name. Let's not get into it. It didn't matter. His hips ground against me, burying his dick deep as he came with a grunt. Yes. For all his honeyed words and carrying on, he'd come grunting at me. Pure romance.

This was why people shouldn't get carried away with emotions etcetera. Even if the sex happened to be insanely good. Hormones can make you do stupid things like yelling out names of people you should probably only be friends with. Like, fuck buddies at best. Because once you start getting carried away, things get complicated. When you're all wound up and feeling a million things including horribly exposed.

"You shouted my name," he said almost wonderingly. The idiot.

"Should I have shouted someone else's?" And while my lungs and heart might have been scrambling to catch up, my body was rigid, unyielding. "Put me down."

Prudently, yet tenderly, he did so. "Martha, what are you thinking about?"

"Why do you always ask me that after sex?" I snapped, gathering up my clothing. "It's unnecessary. The whole point of sex is not to think."

For a moment, there was silence.

"What?" I snapped again.

"Is this about you saying my name?"

"No."

"You sure about that?"

"Yes."

"So it's about intimacy in general, then?"

I cringed. "Seriously?"

God knows where my panties had gone. Doubtless the completely wrong person would find them tomorrow and I'd be in for another round of humiliation. I pulled on the shorts then got busy collecting the shoes and socks. I could walk back to my room barefoot. It wasn't like it'd matter.

Meanwhile, he just stood there bare-ass naked, arms crossed, watching me.

"What?" I asked, getting down on my hands and knees to try and find the fucking underwear. Shit. They'd disappeared. And he'd been totally right about the rough flooring. My back or hands and knees would have been shredded. Of course his being right and caring about me only made things worse. "Are you going to get dressed? And why are you giving me that look?"

"What look am I giving you exactly?"

"Blank face, but pissed-off eyes. It's the one you use when you're angry, but pretending as if you're trying to hide it."

"Well, Martha," he said, pausing to pick up his shorts and pull them on, "I was giving you that particular look because we just had great sex, and before I can even catch my breath, you're suddenly being a raging bitch. What I'm wondering is, why?"

"Why you're bothering with me or why I'm being a bitch?" I asked, rising back to my feet. "Because I have a well-known reputation for being a bitch so I don't see that stopping anytime soon. As for the other, there's a very simple answer. We can just stop. We've had a few good fucks. Might as well end it while we're ahead, right?"

He just blinked.

"What? What is it now?"

"Are you honestly that afraid of feeling something for me?"

I set my jaw, but it didn't help. Neither did staring at the stupid floor.

"C'mon," he said, voice softer. "Look at me."

Surly as shit, I did so. God knows why.

"Tell me what's wrong."

My shoulders slumped. "I can't find my panties."

He exhaled and looked around, inspecting the room. Next he crossed over to a collection of dumbbells and hooked my black thong with his index finger. Trust him to find them immediately. I held out my hand to take them, but he drew me in close.

"What else is wrong?" he asked.

And the words were there, but actually speaking them…

Arms wrapped around me, holding me carefully. Like I was delicate and might break. Like I had cracks in me already. "You can tell me, love. It's okay."

My throat tightened, eyes hurting. "The last time I was doing stupid things like yelling people's names out during sex and getting all overemotional, everything went wrong. I made it go wrong."

"You and Dave?"

I nodded, cheek pressed against his chest.

"That was a long time ago," he said. "I think you're a bit wiser now, don't you?"

"No."

He rubbed my back, kissing the top of my head. God, he was so good at this stuff and I was so not. My arms clung to him. "Martha, no matter whose fault it was, I know you got hurt last time. And I can tell you for a fact that I'm not going to hurt you. That is *not* going to happen. But only you can decide if I'm worth the risk."

"I don't want to hurt you either." I hated the thought. He was such a good man. And this was all getting so complicated so quickly.

"Then don't," he said. "It's that simple."

I sniffled, taking a deep breath. "Honestly, Sam. It's barely been twenty-four hours. How could things possibly get this difficult in such a short amount of time? It's crazy."

Without a word, he picked me up, sitting me on his lap on the bench. "Not really. I think we've been dancing around each other for a long time. By the time we finally got together, it was bound to be...well..."

"I guess so."

"A bit more complicated then you intended, hmm?"

"You could say that."

"Do you really want to just stop?"

"No." I leaned my head against his shoulder, getting comfortable. Not hiding. Something other than that.

"All right then."

"All right then," I mimicked in a deep voice. "You're so full of shit, pretending to go along with everything. 'You're in charge, Martha.' 'Whatever you say, Martha.'"

"I'm your servant in all things, love," he said, the smile obvious in his voice. "I just try to help you along occasionally is all."

"Yeah, right." I sighed. "I'm not just using you for sex. I don't know what it is, but...anyway."

"Well, I'm certainly glad to hear you can admit it. Even if you are describing us as *but anyway*."

"Shut up," I grumbled.

He just laughed. Bastard.

CHAPTER SEVEN

"You cannot be serious."

Sam smirked, keeping his gaze on the road. And looking very handsome in blue jeans, a gray T-shirt, and his black leather jacket. Though in all fairness, he made most things look hot. Despite my best efforts, I'd come to realize it was just a me and him state of being. The effect the man had on me had sadly, steadily escalated over the last few days of sleeping together. (Out in the pool house, not in my room. Gibby loved surprising me with an early wake-up and no child needed to see that much skin so soon in life.) You'd think us fucking like rabbits would have calmed things down, satiated the hunger, so to speak. But no. The desire for Sam was like a constant hum beneath my skin, a warmth spreading through my body at the mere thought of him or the sound of his name. Just as bad as some sappy love song. All in all, very disturbing. And yet...

"Lizzy, no," I said, turning in the passenger seat to give her a glare.

"Martha, yes." She flipped her hair, checking her makeup in a compact. Then she rested her arm on the empty kid's car seat at her side. "This is happening. I mean, I told you, we're going out for drinks. Isn't that what I said, Sam?"

"That is indeed exactly what you said, Mrs. Nicholson," he dutifully answered.

I gasped. "Don't you dare take her side."

"Sorry, love."

"You two are so cute together." Liz grinned. "Have I mentioned that? Because you are, you're absolutely adorable."

"Shut up," I grouched.

The woman in the back seat just happy-sighed. "Anyhoo, as I was saying. It's too late to back out now. I've told them you're coming. You don't want to look like you're scared of them or something, do you? Big bad Martha afraid of having drinks with the wives."

"Why, you little..."

The executive protection officer chuckled all amused-like. Until he caught me glaring at him out of the corner of his eye. "Sorry. That just slipped out."

"You seem to be spending a lot of time in this relationship apologizing, Sam," Lizzy said. "Is that going to wind up being a problem somewhere down the track?"

He licked his fine lips. "I've made peace with it, Mrs. Nicholson. After all, every relationship has its compromises."

"Fair enough."

"I hate you both." I stared out at the passing lights of inner city Portland. Furious yet resigned. Mostly furious. Resigned was just the side dish and boy, did it taste bitter.

"So much negative emotion," Liz tutted. "It's not good for you, Martha."

"What isn't good for me is being lied to and manipulated. You know full well the last fucking thing I'd ever want to do is to go for drinks *there*."

"Which is why I feel it's time for like...a healing, you know?" She nodded all sage-like. "Just get all of the bad history out and deal with it. I think after tonight, you're going to feel much better about things. Don't you think so, Sam?"

He winced. "I'd prefer not to express an opinion on this particular occasion if you don't mind."

"Of course."

At times such as this, it would have been nice to speak more than one language. Because swearing in English didn't quite cover it. My sister-in-law deserved to have her ass handed to her in at least three or four different cultures.

The luxury SUV pulled up to the curb and he took in the passing flow of pedestrians and traffic. Night or day, the Pearl District was a popular destination with all its bars and shops.

"Here we are," said Sam, calm and cool as can be. As per usual. "Let me get the doors."

But I opened my own car door and Liz did likewise. "We're fine, Sam. Relax."

A line had embedded itself between his brows when we met him on the sidewalk. But he got to open the door to the building for us after inputting a security code. That seemed to make him happier.

"You look beautiful tonight," he said in a low voice as I walked past. "That dress is...let's just say that keeping my mind on work might be a little more difficult than usual."

I smiled. "Thank you. You look rather handsome yourself."

At the elevators, we stood in silence. It was a nice apartment building. Very expensive looking with an Art Deco front and white marble entry. Top of the line security system, no doubt. About what you'd expect, given David and Mal both resided there. In the lift, Sam slipped his hand into mine, giving my damp fingers a light squeeze. So I was nervous. Who wouldn't be? I tried to smile, but it didn't quite work. Given tonight would probably feature quite high on my top ten list of hellish situations to be thrown into, I appreciated him not telling me everything would be fine.

"Have you been to David and Ev's place before?" asked Liz.

My face just fell. "You're shitting me. We're not even going to your sister's?"

"Oh, stop worrying, would you?"

Sam's forehead crinkled up with worry lines, his gaze moving between us.

"It's fine," I forced out between gritted teeth. "I'm sure it'll be fine."

His smile wasn't particularly convincing either. "That's my girl."

The hallway ended with a door at either end. Something in my stomach curled in dread as the whole feeling of walking to my doom escalated. No. It would be fine. Show no fear and all that.

Ev answered the door with a big smile, blond hair bouncing along with her tits. Christ, the girl was bouncy. David really had gone from night to day with his choices in women when he replaced me with her. Not that we hadn't been broken for years yaddah yaddah. But he had been my first boyfriend. My first everything. I felt entitled to an opinion.

"Liz, Sam, Martha," she said, her smile only appearing slightly strained at the end. "Welcome, come on in. Lena and Anne are already here."

Sam nodded. "Mrs. Ferris."

The floors were wooden and painted a shiny black, the walls a crisp white. It made for a cool contrast. Dark wood dining table with a huge white leather couch and olive throw cushions. Nice. On a low coffee table, imported beer and a couple of wine bottles sat in buckets of ice.

"Help yourself," said Ev, plonking her ass down on the couch. "You're not going to hide out in the kitchen for once, Sam? That's very brave of you."

"You're not worried you'll get estrogen poisoning, are you?" asked Jimmy's wife, Lena. Dark hair, glasses, pretty. Though they were all pretty, to be fair. She had on a bright red T-shirt, ripped black jeans, and a pair of studded Louboutin booties I would kill to own.

"I'm willing to risk it if you don't mind me hanging around." Sam smiled, taking up sentry duty in the corner. Probably because he was worried about me opening my big mouth and saying the wrong thing. Or maybe he was just worried about me in general.

"Just don't report back to the menfolk and we'll be fine."

Sam snorted. "No fear of that."

"He barely tolerates the boys," said Ev. "We're his real favorites. Right, Sam?"

"You have seen straight through my carefully curated façade, Mrs. Ferris."

"Welcome back to town, Martha." Anne sat with a bottle of water in hand. We'd only crossed paths a time or two, but Lizzy's sister and Mal's wife seemed the exact opposite of his own loud and painfully in-your-face personality. The woman came across as quiet, thoughtful, bookish, things like that. So distinctly different to her slightly evil sister as well.

"Thank you." I nodded stiffly, perched on the very end of the sofa. "Nice to be back."

"I hear Gibby is loving having you there."

"God, he is," said Lizzy, shoving a glass of wine at me and mouthing the word "relax."

I just gave her a dirty look. "Aunty Martha is even more popular than the Super Puppies right now."

"Please don't mention those fucking dogs." Lena sighed. "The girls want the show on around the clock. It's driving us insane."

"Shall I sing you the special super puppy friend's amazing song?"

Lizzy opened her mouth in a clear and present threat.

"Depends. Is this your way of begging for the sweet relief of death?"

"I'll hold her down for you," I offered.

"You're on." Lena leaned across the couch, tapping her bottle of beer against my glass. "Don't do it, Liz. You're facing both a mother and a nanny on the edge due to those cute little do-good mongrels."

Liz just smiled. "Yeah, I hate them too."

"It's that bad?" asked Anne, nose wrinkled.

"Just wait. Little kids fixate worse than serial killers."

Anne's eyes widened.

"Remember when we couldn't find Mister Elephant so he refused to sleep for two days?" Liz shook her head. "I can still hear the pitiful wails and glass-shattering screams echoing in my head."

"Kids are the best," confirmed Lena.

"You can't even imagine the love you're capable of until you have your own child."

"Because Lord knows, they will test you."

Liz and Lena raised their drinks in toast to each other. And having now spent quality time around small children, I sympathized. I really did. But I also kept glancing at Evelyn, relaxing with a beer. Good God, this was awkward. If they were waiting for me to relax, I might as well just stick a straw in one of the bottles of wine and start drinking. Because that's what it would take. After this, Lizzy wasn't even getting coal for Christmas. Broccoli maybe. Or no, a despicably ugly outfit which I would pretend to be all excited about and insist on her wearing somewhere public. Not a bad idea.

"So," said Ev. "Whose life do we dissect first?"

Anne grinned. "Yes! Give me the gossip, ladies."

"Martha has news." Faintly malicious delight filled Lizzy's eyes. "Martha's been very busy."

"You really do have a death wish," I said, glancing tellingly at Sam. He, meanwhile, stared serenely out at nothing. Obviously ignoring the chatter entirely. Thank God. And I did feel better with him close, dammit.

"Leave Sam and Martha alone," chided Ev. "You know what it's like when you first get together…it's special. They probably want to keep it to themselves."

Lizzy rolled her eyes dramatically. "Puh-lease. You were straight on the phone to your bestie Lauren giving her all the juicy details when you and David finally got on with it. She told me."

"Oh, I was not."

"Liar. Spill it, Martha."

Ev shook her head. "Liz, she feels uncomfortable enough just being here."

Silence descended. Thick, heavy, and embarrassing as all hell. I could feel all of the curious glances and awkward side-eyes. The women were just as bad as the fucking men. Honest to God, Lizzy's outfit was going to be the ugliest thing in creation for making me sit through this.

"Let's deal with that then because I don't get out often enough for tonight to be all shitty and awkward." Lena sat up, picking the knife off the cheese platter and hitting her glass with it. "This is the first break I've had from potty-training and picking up toys in ages and I'd say Martha and Lizzy are in a similar situation."

"Adult time is precious," agreed Liz. "Though I'm loving being back at college."

"Yes, I want to hear about that," said Ev, all enthusiasm. "I swear, my brain just gets stuck in barista mode if I don't open a book often enough."

"How's the second coffee shop you bought going?"

"Really well." Ev beamed. "But first we need to deal with this. You're right, Lena."

Oh no.

With a deep breath, Ev faced me head on. "Martha, the past is the past and I'd rather all of that crap got left back there forgotten, if you know what I mean? Like, life is too short. I vote for letting it go, okay?"

My jaw hung low. "Um. Okay?"

"Great." She nodded. "What next?"

"That easily?" I asked, needing to be sure.

She shrugged. "Why should it be hard? David and I are happy. You've apparently moved on with Sam. I assume you have no nefarious plans to mess with my relationship or anything?"

"No," I answered honestly. "None."

"Exactly. You're past that. And it all happened years ago, anyway."

I looked to Sam and he nodded encouragingly.

"Great."

"You don't want me to apologize or something?" I asked, cocking my head.

"I don't know." She wrinkled her lips. "Would you mean it?"

The question required serious consideration. Deep down inside, I harbored no real hate for the woman. If anything, a lingering sense of embarrassment coated those memories. Years ago, I'd tried to break her and her new husband up. That he'd once been my long-time boyfriend didn't really matter. Not really. Without a doubt, it'd been a heinous thing to do. Yet here she was allowing me into her home.

Highly doubtful if the situations were reversed I'd ever be that nice.

"We weren't friends at the time and I didn't owe you anything," I said, choosing my words with care. "But I do regret trying to upset your and David's happiness, if that counts?"

"Okay. I can live with that."

"Yay," said Liz quietly.

Except then I thought about it some more. This was my chance to get rid of this situation entirely. Over in the corner, I could feel how Sam had tensed. How he watched me carefully. While I wasn't going to prostate myself to make him happy, it seemed stupid not to swallow my pride just a little and admit to past mistakes. I'd come back in search of family. Some sense of belonging. Maybe this might be part of it here.

Decision made. "No, look…it was a shit thing to do. I highly doubt we're ever going to be best buddies or anything. But I was out of line and I'm sorry."

Ev paused, surprised. "Thank you, Martha. I forgive you."

Done. I took a sip of wine.

"This is so beautiful." Lena wiped a fake tear from her eye with much drama. "You two are consciously coupling and I feel like there should be violins or something. Rose petals drifting down from the ceiling."

Ev threw a cushion at her and the woman's wine sloshed over the rim of her glass. I couldn't help but smile. It was a good hit. And across from me, even I could admit that Lizzy's self-satisfied expression was probably well earned. So I didn't throw anything at her. I might not even give her the wardrobe equivalent of cow dung for Christmas. Maybe. Perhaps having female friends that were more than just casual acquaintances wouldn't be the worst thing ever.

"So you two are friends now?" asked Anne, sounding slightly

astounded.

"Sure," said Ev. "Why not? And now how about we talk about why Anne is only drinking water. That's what I want to discuss next."

"Oooh." Lena chuckled. "I totally missed that. Oh my God."

"I might just go wait in the kitchen," said Sam, slipping away. But not before giving me a look full of pride. Easing back further in the seat, I watched him go with a smile.

CHAPTER EIGHT

"No-no-no!"

"Yes-yes-yes," I shouted back because mature. "One tiny weeny little cube of carrot, then you get a spoonful of spaghetti. That was the deal."

Gibby laughed and shook his head, delighted with our game. Meanwhile, Ben just sat opposite, smiling. Probably because he wasn't the one having to convince the kid to eat something healthy. As battles of wills went, meal times rocked. For Gib, not for me. I usually lost. Though I'd found that by confiscating the dish and spoon early on, less food got thrown around. A good thing for everyone involved, but mostly me.

"You've been behaving so well all morning." I shook my head. "This is sad. You're giving Aunty Martha sad face. I hope you're proud of yourself, young man."

Gibby clapped his hands. "Yes!"

"Of course you are."

"He gets that from you." Ben smiled around his cup of coffee. "Little horns come out of his head sometimes, too. It's all from you, sister."

"Dream on. He's your child, through and through."

"Darling, eat the piece of carrot," he said, turning his attention back to his son. "C'mon now, rabbits eat carrot."

"Wabbit?" asked Gib from his high chair, interested suddenly.

I nodded. "And rabbits can hop like insanely well. They can jump so high! You want to be cool like a rabbit, don't you?"

After a moment's thought, the child opened his mouth. I wasted no time shovelling the carrot in. Success.

"That being said"—I continued with the adult portion of the conversation—"your wife is pretty damn evil too."

"Damn," mumbled Gib around a mouthful of now orange mush.

Ben and I both winced, then shrugged. He'd copied worse before. He'd copy worse again. Given he lived surrounded by rock stars half the time, it was amazing the small child didn't already swagger and swear in five languages.

"I had nothing to do with her dragging you to David and Ev's last night," said Ben. "Though I hear it turned out all right."

"Apparently in my thirties I am in fact capable of occasional small acts of maturity. Who could have guessed?"

"Good for you."

"Meh. Whatever."

He just smiled.

"How is getting down Adam's tracks going?"

"Yeah, good. Kid's got potential, I'm telling you."

"I believe you. I've heard him, and I'm sure you'll do a great job with the album."

"Thanks. We're not the only ones who think he's going places, either," he said. "He's having a meeting out by the pool with Adrian right now."

I blinked. "Wait. You left Adam alone with Adrian?"

Ben blinked back at me. "Why wouldn't I?"

"Because Adam is an innocent young fool and Adrian will have him signing his life and rights away in two-point-zero seconds flat?" I dropped the spoon, wiping my hands on a cloth. "Holy crap, Ben. How could you?"

"Crap," said Gib.

"Look after your son while I take care of the other child," I ordered, rising to my feet and making for the nearest hallway.

"He's twenty-five. He can look after himself."

"Oh, as if."

At which point, I broke out into a run. God only knows what Adrian would have already talked the kid into. Lifelong musical servitude and a commission that would make a grown man cry. Sure enough, Adrian had dressed for the kill in a gray suit with one of his dumbass ugly, heavy gold chains around his neck. They really didn't work for him.

Adam was scratching his head, staring at the thick wad of paperwork laid on the table. "I just really want to play my music, you know?"

"Of course you do," said Adrian, passing the boy a pen.

"Stop!" I yelled, pulling out one of the fancy chairs beside Adam. "Don't you sign a damn thing, you idiot."

"Martha." Adrian's friendly smile turned feral. "How nice to see you. Is there a problem?"

"Adam, eyes on me." The time spent dealing with a toddler had not gone to waste at all. "The guys have their own lawyers go over anything Adrian presents them with and never accept his first offer when contract time rolls around. Do you understand me?"

The manager's laugh sounded both forced and fake. "But that's a different situation. Adam here is just starting out and quite honestly, he's fortunate I'm even—"

I held up my hand. "Shut it. You've had your chance to speak. It's my turn now."

"Well, what do you think I should do?" asked Adam with a heavy sigh.

"This might be the first offer you've received, but it's not going to be the only one."

"Maybe."

I looked to heaven. Honestly. "Try definitely. You're talented. Why do you think he flew up from L.A. to impress you with his bling?"

Adrian's hand flew to his chunky chain in mock outrage. Or maybe it was real. Whatever. His teeth and suntan sure as hell weren't. Scarily white veneers and orange skin he most definitely had not been born with. Ugh.

"Anyone who would encourage you to sign something without legal advice is not someone you want to work with."

"I was trying to save the boy money," said Adrian.

"Yet an unscrupulous business person in this position might try to get him on a hook with a ridiculous offer he'd regret in the first five minutes. Don't you think?"

Adam's mouth edged down. "Shit. Now I don't know what to do."

"Ben will lend you his lawyer. Don't worry." I patted the poor boy on the arm. "I get that it seems exciting and a good opportunity. But you never rush in without knowing exactly what you're signing up for. Never. Are we understood?"

He tipped his chin in acknowledgement.

"Are you seriously going to take the advice of a woman wearing a T-shirt covered in cartoon dogs with spaghetti in her hair?" spluttered Adrian.

I groaned and bent my head. "I thought I got it all out. Adam, can you please?"

"Sure." He started picking among the strands of hair. Ah, the glamour.

"And they're Super Puppies, not dogs. Get it right."

"Can't you just be my manager?" asked Adam, still busy with my hair. Guitarists' fingers really came in useful sometimes. "You're scary like him, but in a way I can handle. I mean, I can talk to you without getting completely fucking confused and wound up about everything. Plus, those festivals you recommended the other day would all be perfect. If you could get me booked."

"You know, I bet I could."

He grinned. "That would be awesome. Ah, think I got all the noodles. There's a bit of sauce in there you'll need to wash out."

"Thanks," I said. "Look, I haven't really given serious thought to managing you. But let me mull it over, all right?"

On the other side of the table, Adrian's face had turned an unfortunate shade of purple. "You want Martha to manage you? Are you out of your mind? She's a secretary, for heaven's sake."

"Executive personal assistant, thank you," I snapped. "And an extremely experienced one. So if you think during the years I worked with the band I wasn't all over everything the guys did making sure they weren't getting ripped off or messed around with, you are kidding yourself."

"What exactly are you insinuating?"

"Oh, don't get litigious," I said. "You're a great manager, Adrian. I'm not denying it. But you're not necessarily the best fit for every performer. No manager possibly could be."

The man's eyebrows merged into one flat pissed-off line.

"Whatever Adam does, he needs to take the time to ensure he's well informed as to his responsibilities and the consequences of any contract he signs." I crossed my arms. "Wouldn't you agree, Adrian?"

"W-well, of course no one wants to take advantage of him."

"Of course not."

"Right. Okay," said Adam, exhaling hard. "I'll read through it all and get some legal advice then get back to you. Thank you."

Adrian just grunted. Talk about being an unhappy camper.

I, however, smiled with delight and Adam seemed much more relaxed. Doing good deeds didn't suck nearly as much as I'd thought it would. Besides, maybe I would make a good manager. Serious thought about the idea was definitely required.

The problems associated with possibly dating (or whatever we were doing) a bodyguard became very clear four days later. Four days during which I hadn't seen Sam. Not even once.

Rumors about the new album were running rife. And paparazzi had taken to following the band members and their partners, trying to get the gossip. To make things even worse, Jimmy's old flame, a big-time Hollywood actress, had just announced her engagement. So they wanted a statement from the singer about that too.

One overzealous paparazzo in particular had been a thorough pain in the ass. The guy was way too gung-ho about his job, if repeatedly grabbing the back of David's shirt and stepping in front of cars to try and get a picture were any indication. Spread thin trying to keep an eye on the still lurking photographer/stalker, more security came on board. Things turned intense.

Something I could have dealt with just fine, if Sam hadn't up and completely disappeared on me. Apart from a text. One damn text.

"Wat den?" asked one of Jimmy and Lena's twins. Not sure which one. I could never keep their names straight.

Me, the children, and one idiot drummer were sitting among a wide assortment of toys in the corner of the band's practice room again. Meanwhile, Ben and Jimmy were busy inside the studio. David sat on one of the couches with a guitar resting in his lap and paper and pen at his side. He was lost in his own little world, which tended to happen when he wrote songs.

Since each other's houses were considered some of the only safe places to visit, we'd all been hanging out together often. Fine with me. It kept them all happy and occupied to play together. The children and the band members.

Gib removed his thumb from his mouth. "Pwada."

"That's right," I said, giving the child a high five for excellence. "Then, the Super Puppy team put on their new season Prada sunglasses and ran off into the sunset to frolic and play or whatever. Knowing that through their awesome styling tips and quite adequate life-saving rescue mission, the hamsters would all happily live to see another day. The end."

The questioning twin just blinked at me. Guess she wasn't used to my style of story-telling yet.

"Have to admit," said Lena, studying her state-of-the-art camera, flicking through shots no doubt, "I was really worried there for a while when the hamster couldn't decide what cut of jeans to get."

"Flares was a daring option, but I really do believe they're making a comeback," I agreed. "Harry the hamster's going to have all the street cred."

Mal nodded, finishing up doing a third tiny plait on the head of one of the twins. "Your story had me on the edge of my seat, Marty. Which isn't easy considering I'm sitting on the ground. Okay, another successful hairdo. Let's hear it for Uncle Mal!"

All of the children clapped their hands.

"M-A-L, he's the best. Yes, he is." The drummer had a full cheer routine with hand motions and all going on. "Yay for Uncle Mal!"

Lena just shook her head. "Martha, come see this one. I think it might make a good cover shot."

"Coming." I hopped up.

"Can I stop staring slightly broodingly yet meaningfully at the wall now?" asked Adam.

"No, stay there," ordered Lena. "The light's perfect."

On top of deciding to become Adam's manager (with Sam MIA I had plenty of time to think deep thoughts), I'd temporarily played the part of his stylist today. Mal had offered, but we'd let him experiment on the children instead. Hence the current array of crazy hairdos on everyone under three. The second twin had an attempt at a mohawk and Gib's hair had been spiked. Lots of hair products were involved in both. Lizzy or Ben could do bath time tonight. My nephew had a tendency to howl like a banshee when hair wash time came around. No way would I be volunteering.

"Nice," I said, checking out the picture.

"The wall will be out of shot, but you see what I mean about the light?"

I nodded. "The shadows work. Very emotive."

"I feel like an idiot," mumbled Adam in his black shirt and distressed jeans. We'd nailed the outfit. It really made the most of his messy hair and lanky frame.

"And you look like one," said Mal. "Rest assured."

Dave chuckled. "Get used to it. Photo shoots are always awkward as hell. Remember that time they tried to put me in red sequinned pants?"

"That was special. Though the tartan suit was my favorite."

"Actually, I didn't mind it."

"Davie, you are such a show pony."

"Afternoon, ladies and gentleman." A familiar deep voice entered the room. "And children, of course."

My head shot up, eyes narrowing.

Sam stopped cold. "My love, it's good to see you. Is something wrong?"

"It is good to see you," I said, abandoning the camera and heading straight for the bodyguard. "Surprising to see you even."

"What's with that tone of voice?"

"Guess."

"You're very, very angry." He slid an arm around my waist. I didn't knock it away. Not yet at least.

"Four days, Sam. Four days with barely a fu…" I looked down just in time to catch Gibby attaching himself to my leg. "Freaking word."

"Sam-Sam-Sam." The small child grinned, reaching out to pat the black slacks of the big man. The one in seriously deep shit.

"Hello, Gibby." Sam smiled then exhaled. "Martha, I've been busy at Jim and Lena's. I texted to tell you that."

"One single text. That's the best you could manage."

His Adam's apple bobbed. "Ah…"

I said nothing.

"I should have at least made the effort to call you. You're right."

"Keep going," I encouraged. Still not smiling.

"It's possible I have some workaholic tendencies. And well, we've been very busy…and, um…" His gaze darted around the room, seeking inspiration or pleading for help from the other adults. So nice to have everyone witnessing yet another dramatic moment.

"May I remind you that you said working twenty-four-seven no longer appealed to you," I said. "That you wanted to make time for more in your life. Like a relationship, perhaps?"

His mouth opened slightly, but nothing came out.

"Given the old saying, begin as you mean to go on, does disappearing with barely a word for four days sound like a relationship to you?"

"I definitely should have made more of an effort to stay in contact with you." He licked his lips. "It was an error. I can see that now."

"And the next time there's an emergency situation?"

"I'll call?"

"Not good enough," I said, turning away.

"Love…"

"If you want me to be all in on this, then you need to make an effort to be there. Things will always come up, needing your attention. I get that." I attempted to smooth down Gibby's hair a little. It didn't work, but it was quite calming. "But you can't talk marriage and children to me, even jokingly, and then disappear for days."

"I wasn't joking," said Sam, voice low and serious.

"Marriage and children?" The whites of David's eyes seemed huge. "Really?"

Sam made a noise in his throat. "Yes, Dave. I love her. Is that a problem?"

Holy shit. I just kind of froze.

"No. Just a…no," said David. "You two? Right. Um, none of my business. Sorry, I—"

"Stop speaking now, man," wisely suggested Mal.

"Yep."

Hands cupping my face, Sam frowned. "Love, I'm sorry. You're right, I messed this up and I did want to slow down on the working around the clock and having no life. So you're in charge, you tell me how to fix it and I will."

"Marty's in charge?" asked Mal, tone somewhat astounded. "Seriously, man?"

"Shh," whisper-hissed Lena.

I did my best to ignore them all while Sam stood in front of me, waiting. Because I was in charge. At least right now. This required some thought. "I don't want to run your life, but I do want to be a part of it. I know that much. I also know that if you keep doing the same job you're doing now, at the rate you're doing it, this is going to keep happening."

He nodded. "You want me to consider retiring?"

"No," I said, shaking my head slightly. "You're like me, I think. Without something to keep your brain occupied you'd slowly go insane."

"Probably."

"Definitely."

"What then?" he asked. "Time to consider a change of vocation?"

"But you're good at this and you enjoy it. Hell, you're the best."

"Hell," repeated Gibby, still clinging to my leg.

"So, my thought is, what if you went into business for yourself?" I asked, turning the problem over inside my head. "What if instead of being the guy standing out on the driveway at all hours, you were the person in the office managing everything and only on site some of the time?"

Speculation filled Sam's gaze. "You know…that's not a bad idea."

I smiled.

"I could start my own security business." He placed a sweet kiss upon my lips. "This is why you're in charge, love. Brains and beauty, they're a lethal mix."

Mal cleared his throat. "Sorry to interrupt, but…you'd still work for us right, Sam, man?"

"I'd work with you, Malcolm, as a contractor. And charge you a very generous rate."

"A reasonable rate," I corrected. "Let's not go overboard."

"Huh," said the drummer. "Okay then. Carry on."

"When you're not busy with Adam, perhaps you could help me?" asked Sam. "Setting things up is going to be quite involved."

"Really? You want me to be involved?"

"Absolutely."

I grinned. "I'd be delighted to."

"No more disappearing, I promise," he said, kissing me again. Deeper and more thoroughly this time. Yet without squishing the small child still attached to me. He kissed me like he'd missed me even more than I'd missed him. Because of course I had. Dammit. Maybe things would be okay after all.

When we finally came up for air, I still had the grin on my face. "You said you loved me."

"Why else would I call you love, hmm?" He smiled back. "You're not even freaking out about it, quite surprisingly."

I shrugged. "Eh. With all that time to think things through, I realized I wouldn't have been half as mad about you going MIA unless there was actually something meaningful going on between us."

"Why, that's very brave of you, love."

"Thanks. I thought so."

EPILOGUE

"We're late," I panted, bent over my office desk. "Hurry up."

"You were late. I just came to get you. Then I saw how you were dressed."

Sam did some swivel type motion with his hips and holy shit. I saw stars. Sparkling, swirling big-ass stars. With my dress hitched up around my waist, his cock resumed pounding into me, driving me out of my everloving mind. My insides tightened, legs trembling.

"That's it, love," he ground out. "Nearly there."

"Fuck, Sam!"

The man in question grunted, managing another couple of thrusts before following me over the edge. That sweet lethargy combined with an awesome chemical high filled my body, making it hard to move. Lungs heaving, heart stuttering, I just half lay, half stood there. Holy shit. Talk about breaking in the office section of our new home. Nothing like a quick orgasm to make you ready to party.

"Still alive, love?" he asked, pulling my panties back into place and straightening my skirt. The man was good with his hands in all sorts of useful ways.

"Mm-hmm."

"Everyone's waiting downstairs," he said.

"I know, I know. Just had some urgent emails to answer and Adam is just...being Adam."

"The boy's a little out of control since he hit the bigtime."

I frowned, slowly straightening. "That's an understatement. But Ziggy's on him so our rock 'n roll prodigy shouldn't get into much mischief...tonight at least."

"Let me see." He turned me to face him, looking over my makeup and hair. "Still perfect."

"Yeah, but you say that when I have bed hair and morning breath."

"Not my fault you're so beautiful."

"You're awfully good for my ego."

"When it comes to you, I live to serve." He brought my left hand to his lips, giving the monster-size rock on my ring finger a smile. Because bigger is always better.

"I love you," I whispered.

"I love you too. Why are we whispering?"

I laughed. "No idea. Let's go do this thing."

Sam's business had been in operation for almost six months and was a total success. We'd both put in some serious hours along the way, but it'd been worth it. Turned out he had a gift for training up the new executive protection officers and managing in general. Our team was still small at present, but in high demand. Though the Stage Dive family tended to keep us busy. And Adam, of course.

As for me, between Adam's overnight success, finding our own place, and helping Sam get things going, I'd been kept plenty busy. There'd been no time for Hawaii or anywhere else for that matter. So about a month ago, I'd informed my big, strong, and very understanding man that it was time for some bling and he'd delivered. Boy, had he delivered. No idea when we'd have time to plan a wedding. Maybe we'd stick with group tradition and go get hitched in Vegas.

Downstairs, the whole crew was assembled. Jimmy and Ben were keeping an eye on the assorted children busy at play while Lena and Lizzy caught up over beers. Gib's box of toys in the corner had been one of our first investments. Because having a three-year-old running around your house bored is just asking for trouble. Having three of them with nothing to play with would be an outright nightmare. And while I might not be Gib's nanny any longer, he still visited once a week for a sleep-over so his parents could get some adult time together. Also so Gib, Sam, and I could have our bonding time, of course.

Ev and David were preparing pizzas in the kitchen. God only knew what would be on them. When it came to pizza toppings during our girls' nights, I'd learned to just let the woman do her thing. It had taken a slightly tense discussion/argument between us regarding broccoli and zucchini. Because honest to God, who the hell puts those things on a pizza? I mean, honestly. It still blew my mind. But so long as pepperoni continued to be provided, I decided to let it go. So yes, we might occasionally still butt heads over small silly things. But it generally all worked out just fine. Due to age, wisdom, or being too damn worn out running our respective businesses to bother stressing...who knows? Ev and I were at peace. Even David and I basically got along.

On the long gray suede couch, Anne enjoyed the housewarming by sitting and doing her best to relax. Something probably not easily managed, care of Mal ever so gently tapping out drum beats with his fingers on her huge pregnant belly. Her tolerance levels were pretty much superior to mine in every way. Anne was a saint as far as I was concerned and the designer baby suits I had stashed away waiting for the delivery were too cute for words. Sweet of her to give me another reason to shop. The two women I'd really bonded with, however, were Lena and Lizzy. They were both slightly evil and sarcastic, two qualities I appreciated greatly. And if I needed something, they were there for me. Ditto to me being there for them. Because relationships were totally a give and take type situation.

It might have taken me a while to figure it out, but family and friends mattered. Family, friends, and my man. And our house.

"You're smiling," said Sam, slipping an arm around my waist as we stood at the bottom of the stairs.

"That's because I'm happy."

"Oh? And why is that?" he asked, pretending ignorance.

I shrugged, nestling in closer to him. Turned out I was a cuddler after all. "Because life is good."

"I'm glad, love. I'm very glad indeed," he said. "Welcome home."

THE END

Sign up for the 1001 Dark Nights Newsletter
and be entered to win a Tiffany Key necklace.

There's a contest every month!

Go to www.1001DarkNights.com to subscribe.

As a bonus, all subscribers will receive a free copy of
Discovery Bundle Three
Featuring stories by
Sidney Bristol, Darcy Burke, T. Gephart
Stacey Kennedy, Adriana Locke
JB Salsbury, and Erika Wilde

Discover 1001 Dark Nights Collection Five

Visit www.1001DarkNights.com for more information.

BLAZE ERUPTING by Rebecca Zanetti
Scorpius Syndrome/A Brigade Novella

ROUGH RIDE by Kristen Ashley
A Chaos Novella

HAWKYN by Larissa Ione
A Demonica Underworld Novella

RIDE DIRTY by Laura Kaye
A Raven Riders Novella

ROME'S CHANCE by Joanna Wylde
A Reapers MC Novella

THE MARRIAGE ARRANGEMENT by Jennifer Probst
A Marriage to a Billionaire Novella

SURRENDER by Elisabeth Naughton
A House of Sin Novella

INKED NIGHT by Carrie Ann Ryan
A Montgomery Ink Novella

ENVY by Rachel Van Dyken
An Eagle Elite Novella

PROTECTED by Lexi Blake
A Masters and Mercenaries Novella

THE PRINCE by Jennifer L. Armentrout
A Wicked Novella

PLEASE ME by J. Kenner
A Stark Ever After Novella

WOUND TIGHT by Lorelei James
A Rough Riders/Blacktop Cowboys Novella®

STRONG by Kylie Scott
A Stage Dive Novella

DRAGON NIGHT by Donna Grant
A Dark Kings Novella

TEMPTING BROOKE by Kristen Proby
A Big Sky Novella

HAUNTED BE THE HOLIDAYS by Heather Graham
A Krewe of Hunters Novella

CONTROL by K. Bromberg
An Everyday Heroes Novella

HUNKY HEARTBREAKER by Kendall Ryan
A Whiskey Kisses Novella

THE DARKEST CAPTIVE by Gena Showalter
A Lords of the Underworld Novella

Discover 1001 Dark Nights Collection One

Visit www.1001DarkNights.com for more information.

FOREVER WICKED by Shayla Black
CRIMSON TWILIGHT by Heather Graham
CAPTURED IN SURRENDER by Liliana Hart
SILENT BITE: A SCANGUARDS WEDDING by Tina Folsom
DUNGEON GAMES by Lexi Blake
AZAGOTH by Larissa Ione
NEED YOU NOW by Lisa Renee Jones
SHOW ME, BABY by Cherise Sinclair
ROPED IN by Lorelei James
TEMPTED BY MIDNIGHT by Lara Adrian
THE FLAME by Christopher Rice
CARESS OF DARKNESS by Julie Kenner

Also from 1001 Dark Nights

TAME ME by J. Kenner

Discover 1001 Dark Nights Collection Two

Visit www.1001DarkNights.com for more information.

Discover 1001 Dark Nights Collection Three

Visit www.1001DarkNights.com for more information.

HIDDEN INK by Carrie Ann Ryan
BLOOD ON THE BAYOU by Heather Graham
SEARCHING FOR MINE by Jennifer Probst
DANCE OF DESIRE by Christopher Rice
ROUGH RHYTHM by Tessa Bailey
DEVOTED by Lexi Blake
Z by Larissa Ione
FALLING UNDER YOU by Laurelin Paige
EASY FOR KEEPS by Kristen Proby
UNCHAINED by Elisabeth Naughton
HARD TO SERVE by Laura Kaye
DRAGON FEVER by Donna Grant
KAYDEN/SIMON by Alexandra Ivy/Laura Wright
STRUNG UP by Lorelei James
MIDNIGHT UNTAMED by Lara Adrian
TRICKED by Rebecca Zanetti
DIRTY WICKED by Shayla Black
THE ONLY ONE by Lauren Blakely
SWEET SURRENDER by Liliana Hart

Discover 1001 Dark Nights Collection Four

Visit www.1001DarkNights.com for more information.

ROCK CHICK REAWAKENING by Kristen Ashley
ADORING INK by Carrie Ann Ryan
SWEET RIVALRY by K. Bromberg
SHADE'S LADY by Joanna Wylde
RAZR by Larissa Ione
ARRANGED by Lexi Blake
TANGLED by Rebecca Zanetti
HOLD ME by J. Kenner
SOMEHOW, SOME WAY by Jennifer Probst
TOO CLOSE TO CALL by Tessa Bailey
HUNTED by Elisabeth Naughton
EYES ON YOU by Laura Kaye
BLADE by Alexandra Ivy/Laura Wright
DRAGON BURN by Donna Grant
TRIPPED OUT by Lorelei James
STUD FINDER by Lauren Blakely
MIDNIGHT UNLEASHED by Lara Adrian
HALLOW BE THE HAUNT by Heather Graham
DIRTY FILTHY FIX by Laurelin Paige
THE BED MATE by Kendall Ryan
PRINCE ROMAN by CD Reiss
NO RESERVATIONS by Kristen Proby
DAWN OF SURRENDER by Liliana Hart

Also from 1001 Dark Nights

TEMPT ME by J. Kenner

About Kylie Scott

Kylie is a New York Times and USA Today best-selling author. She was voted Australian Romance Writer of the year, 2013 & 2014, by the Australian Romance Writer's Association and her books have been translated into eleven different languages.

It Seemed Like a Good Idea at the Time
By Kylie Scott
Now Available

"Addictive like all Kylie Scott books, you'll swoon, laugh, ache, put your life on hold, and compulsively read until the wee hours of the night—only to reread the whole thing the next morning. Perfection!" - Katy Evans, *New York Times* bestselling author

Returning home for her father's wedding was never going to be easy for Adele. If being sent away at eighteen hadn't been bad enough, the mess she left behind when she made a pass at her dad's business partner sure was.

Fifteen years older than her, Pete had been her crush for as long as she could remember. But she'd misread the situation—confusing friendliness for undying love. Awkward. Add her father to the misunderstanding, and Pete was left with a broken nose and a business on the edge of ruin. The man had to be just as glad as everyone else when she left town.

Seven years later, things are different. Adele is no longer a kid, but a fully grown adult more than capable of getting through the wedding and being polite. But all it takes is seeing him again to bring back those old feelings.

Sometimes first loves are the truest.

* * * *

In a fair and just world, he'd have looked like shit. The years would have ground him down to all but a shell of his former glory. Of course, this hadn't happened. My luck just wasn't that good.
"You made it," he said, walking barefoot down his front steps.
"Don't sound so surprised. You taught me how to drive."
Pale blue eyes gazed at me flatly. No visible gray in his dark hair. Not yet, anyway.
"Hi, Pete," I said.

Nothing.

"I come in peace."

More of the same.

I climbed out of my car, muscles protesting the movement. My sundress was a crumpled ruin. What had looked hopeful, happy, and bright in the wee hours of the morning didn't hold up so well under the late-afternoon light. A twelve-hour drive from Sydney to South East Queensland's north coast will do that to you. I pushed my sunglasses on top of my head, ready to face my inevitable doom. A light breeze smelled of lush foliage and flowers. And the heat and humidity beat down on me, even with the sun sinking over the hills. I'd forgotten what it was like being in the subtropics during summer. Should have worn more deodorant. Should have faked a communicable disease and stayed home.

"What's it been," he asked, "seven years?"

"About that."

"Thought you were bringing a boyfriend with you."

I paused. Dad must have given him that idea. God knows where Dad, however, had gotten it from. "No. No . . . he's ah, busy."

He looked me over; I guess we were both curious. Last time we'd been in the same room was for my eighteenth birthday party. My hair had been short and my skirt even shorter. What a spectacularly awful night that was. As if he too, remembered, he suddenly frowned, his high forehead filling with lines. Victory! The man definitely had more wrinkles. Unfortunately, they kind of suited him. Enhanced him, even. Bastard.

"Better come inside," he said.

"If you're still pissed at me, then why am I staying here?"

"I am not 'pissed at you.'" His tone was light and just a bit haughty. A sure sign he was pissed. "I just was expecting your boyfriend too, that's all."

I crossed my arms.

"Look," he said, "you're staying here because we're both doing a favor to your dad. I know you haven't met her yet, but Shanti's a nice woman. She's good for him. They make a great couple and I want their wedding to be hassle free."

"I didn't come to cause trouble."

"But with you, from what I recall, it just seems to magically happen." Hands on slim hips, he gave me a grim smile. "It's just a few days, kid. Apparently, your old room is filled with bomboniere, whatever the fuck that is. So you're staying here with me."

I'd heard worse ideas in my life, but not many. Also they usually involved the risk of possible loss of limb, death, or incarceration. I'd tried to talk Dad into alternatives, but he'd stood firm, dammit. "That's kind of you, but not necessary. I'll go get a room at a hotel, this isn't—"

"They're probably booked," he said. "It's peak season so even if you could find somewhere, you'd pay through the roof. Anything nearby is going to already be busy with other wedding guests. Look, your dad wants you close so he can spend some time with you."

I said nothing.

"It's only five days," he repeated in the tone of voice he usually reserved for those dancing on his last damn nerve. "Let's just get through it."

Great. Awesome.

With a nod, I headed for the back of my car. All the better to hide and take a second to pull myself together.

"Did you bring much stuff?" he asked, following.

"No. I've got it."

Except, of course, I didn't. As the hatch opened, he was there, reaching for my suitcase. Muscles flexed in his arms, slightly straining the sleeves of his white T-shirt. The man had always been strong, solid. Unfortunately, he hadn't shrunk any either. I was around average height, but he still had at least half a head on me. Just perfect for looking down and putting me in my place.

"Lock up your car." He headed for the house, tugging my wheeled suitcase behind him. "We might be in the country, but things still happen."

"Yeah, I know to lock up my car," I whisper bitched.

"I heard that."

"I don't give a shit."

He laughed grimly. "Oh, kid, this is going to be fun."

Out of options, I followed. Up the stone steps and into the house. Pete had never been much of a gardener, but someone had done a wonderful job with the grounds. Not that I was willing to say as much. We were apparently at war, and I couldn't even blame him since it was all my fault. God, I hated the old familiar feeling of guilt. Life would be so much easier if I could hate him, push some of the blame his way. But the truth was, he hadn't done a damn thing wrong. Not back then. Not even really now.

My pity party almost distracted me from the house.

"You did it," I breathed, wonder pushing the no-compliment rule straight out of my head. "It's beautiful."

He stopped, blinked. "Yeah."

"Last time I was here you were still living in the shed," I said. "It was just dirt with some pipes and things sticking out of the ground. Now it's finished."

"Parts of it are still a work in progress."

I spun in a slow circle, taking everything in, from the polished wood floors to the gray quartz kitchen located off to one side. A television about the size of a football field hung on one wall, with plush-looking navy couches gathered nearby. A large dining table was made out of a solid slab of wood, the natural edges still rough enough to be decorative. I'd already seen the beginning of that work of art, so I knew he'd made it himself. And the rounded center beam was huge, standing in the middle of the room, holding up the pitched ceiling.

"What is that, two stories high?" I asked, staring up.

"Two and a half."

"Wow. You really did it."

At that, he almost smiled. Almost.

Hallways ran off opposite sides of the great room and there was a wide verandah running the whole length of the building out back. There'd be a barbeque, another dining table and lots of chairs to laze in, and stairs leading down to the pool. I knew it without looking. Just like I knew there'd be the main bedroom with a bathroom and an office off to the right. Two guest bedrooms, a reading nook, and another bathroom off to the left. A long time ago, I'd helped him design this place. We'd worked on it together, a dream house.

"It's perfect," I said quietly.

For a moment, his gaze narrowed. But then his lips returned to their former flat, unhappy state. "Glad you like it. You're in here."

I followed his back into the left wing. The house was amazing. Sadly, my gaze slipped from his wide shoulders, down the length of his spine, to find his gorgeous ass had also lost none of its impact. So unfair. But Pete in jeans always had been a sight to behold. God, his loose-limbed stride. A careless sort of confidence had always just seemed to ooze from the man.

Not that I was looking. Looking was bad.

"This okay?" he asked, throwing open a door.

"Fine. Thanks."

He tapped the top of my luggage. "Where do you want this?"

"I'll handle it."

A nod. "Your dad and Shanti will be over for dinner in a couple of hours."

"Is there anything I can do?"

"No, it's all taken care of." He scratched at his stubble. "Right. Make yourself at home. I'm going to get some work done. Be in the office if you need anything."

I nodded too. Nods were so great. Much better than words.

He stood in the hallway, staring at me for a moment. Not saying anything along the lines of how it was good to see me again. Because that would be a lie.

"Okay, Adele," he finally said, using my name, which was never a good sign. Honestly, I think I actually preferred "kid." Then, thank you baby Jesus, he left.

Carefully, I closed the bedroom door, slumping against it because excessive drama. I'd known coming back was going to be a certain level of hell, but not one quite this deep.

One hundred and twenty hours and counting.

On behalf of 1001 Dark Nights,

Liz Berry and M.J. Rose would like to thank ~

Steve Berry
Doug Scofield
Kim Guidroz
Jillian Stein
InkSlinger PR
Dan Slater
Asha Hossain
Chris Graham
Fedora Chen
Kasi Alexander
Jessica Johns
Dylan Stockton
Richard Blake
and Simon Lipskar

Made in the USA
Middletown, DE
30 October 2018